YUKI: A SNOW WHITE RETELLING

TALES OF AKATSUKI BOOK 2

NICOLETTE ANDREWS

1

Banners snapped in the wind. Thundering hooves raced down the road. The raucous laughter of soldiers filled the air. In times of war, stealth was necessary. But being in neutral territory, and compared to their recent missions, it didn't hurt to let the men ease some of the tension. It was good to see them smile again. It had been too long since they'd had a reason to smile. Hotaru wished he could join them in their revelry, but his thoughts were preoccupied. He scanned the horizon, ever vigilant. Just because they were in friendly territory didn't mean they were completely without risk.

"Ease up, my lord. It's a wife, not a death sentence," his second-in-command said as he pulled up next to Hotaru.

"It is to all the heartbroken girls at the clan!" shouted one of his men.

"At least they have their bastard children to remind them of you," said another.

The others joined in their playful teasing of him and Hotaru forced a smile. If only he were in search of just a wife. It would have been much simpler, and he wouldn't have left their territory. There were plenty of eligible women who would have been more than happy to be his bride. They all knew; they wouldn't have followed him this far if they hadn't. His men were worried, just as he was. This alliance was critical. He couldn't let his fear show. He wanted them to continue to smile.

"I can't waste all my charm on you lot," Hotaru called to his men.

They roared with approval.

The cheers soon died away as the forest came into view. It was as if the air had been sucked out of them. The trees were dense, and growing so close together the trunks were tangled around one another. Their skeletal branches were like clawed hands reaching toward them. Thick, white fog twisted around the bases of barren trees, seeping through the gnarled trunks. Everyone knew these sorts of wild places were the domain of the yokai. Before he had thought those stories were all just peasant's superstition. But he knew better now, and he had learned to show proper respect. If there were any other way around, he would have taken it. But their destination was at the center of this forest.

Their group slowed to a crawl as they delayed the inevitable. Hotaru turned in his saddle to face his men. They all shifted uncomfortably in their seats.

"Keep your eyes open, weapons at hand, and stay on the path," he said.

The road was wide enough for them to travel in twos, and so they lined up as they entered. Hotaru and his second took the lead. The horses nickered with anxiety. Hotaru's had his ears flattened against his skull. They could sense as he could, the otherness of this place. Hotaru surveyed the road ahead, which ended in a thick wall of mist. Everywhere they looked there were long shadows. It was bitingly cold; the spring thaw had only just begun and the road was mired in mud.

Then to his left the bushes rustled, followed by the hasty jostling of men drawing their weapons. Hotaru held up his hand. A fat tanuki waddled out from within the bushes. The raccoon dog turned its masked face toward them. There was an almost human intelligence in its eyes. Of course the creatures were known troublemakers, but legends said they could take the form of humans and delighted in deceiving humans. Hotaru shook his head, this could only be a regular forest creature.

After their brief staring contest, the tanuki disappeared into the forest on the other side of the road and he gave the signal for his men to move on.

It was not long before another tanuki appeared in the pathway.

"This forest is full of tanuki," Hotaru commented as the second one stared at him with clever eyes. This one held his gaze even longer than the first.

The men eyed the surrounding forest, as if they expected a horde of the raccoon dogs to burst out of the shadows and tear the meat from their bones. Hotaru laughed away their fears, more to keep them moving forward than anything. There was a tingling sensation at the back of his mind that told him to keep a look out.

Further down the road, a third tanuki stepped in front of them.

One of his soldiers, fueled by fear and recklessness, shot an arrow at it. Instead of striking it as it should, the tanuki leaped out of the way at just the right moment. And for a split second, Hotaru thought he had seen a straw hat on the creature's head. Before he had time to even process that thought, a woman leaped out of the nearby bushes.

"You're not going to get away from me!" She shouted as she ran past. It seemed she did not notice them at all. And perhaps that was for the best, she looked like a wild creature herself. Her long ebony hair had at one point been tied in a braid, but had mostly come undone, and her feet were bare and caked in mud. Her kimono was splattered and torn and hiked up over her knees.

Hotaru stared after her, mouth slack long after she had disappeared into the forest chasing the tanuki. *Perhaps it was a mistake coming here. I heard these people were strange...* He didn't have a choice. Perhaps the clan leaders were more civilized.

"Let's move out. And do not fire unless I give the order." He looked at the man who had.

The soldier bowed his head in penance. After that there were no more strange encounters and they arrived at the hidden palace. It emerged from the forest and fog like something out of a fairy tale. Large trees flanked it on all sides, and the green tops of the buildings peaked out from behind a wall made of spikes of wood. In the fog it was easy to miss if you did not know what you were looking for.

Hotaru gave the signal for his men to stand down and approached the gate.

"I am Lord Kaedemori, come to see the lord of the clan," he called up.

A guard's head peeked out from over the top of the wall.

"Stand back, the gates are opening."

Hotaru backed away as the massive gate was rolled open and he and his men marched inside. They had announced their visit in advance, and as expected they were greeted by the elders of the clan. At the forefront, a frail man who was swimming in his finely embroidered haori greeted them. He must be the lord's son. Just behind him was a beautiful woman in a bright kimono embroidered with flowers. She could be none other than the lord's daughter and the woman he'd come to marry. Hotaru looked around, expecting the lord of the clan to greet them. But seeing as he wasn't there, Hotaru could only take it as an insult. Negotiations were not going to go as smoothly as he hoped.

He dismounted with a flourish, making sure to give his most charming smile to the onlookers. The lord's daughter hid her smile behind her sleeve. Wooing the lady would be no trouble at all. It was the leader whose respect he'd have to earn.

Hotaru bowed to his hosts. "Thank you for welcoming me here, cousin. I have brought gifts for your father, Lord Fujimori."

He gestured to the trunks of treasures and gifts they had brought. The soldiers unloaded them, placing them in front of the young lord while Hotaru smiled up at them.

The young man's skin was nearly translucent, stretched over his jutting cheekbones and dark circles ringed his eyes. He turned his head to cough.

"It is good to meet you, cousin. But I fear my father is no longer with us."

Hotaru had to keep the surprise from his face. He had not heard that Lord Fujimori had died. It was a small mistake, one that he could quickly rectify.

"I am sorry to hear that. I share your pain; my own father has recently left this world. It is good that we are meeting now, at the beginnings of our individual rule." He addressed the young Lord Fujimori, but it was the young woman who caught his eye. Lady Yuki was just as beautiful as he had been told.

That wasn't always the case for these kinds of rumors. Often times a woman's beauty would be exaggerated as to not scare away potential suitors. Not that it mattered much in this instance. This marriage was a strategic one. He was just fortunate she was so attractive. "It is lovely to meet you and your lovely sister," Hotaru said, bowing his head at the young woman.

"This is not my sister. Yuki should have been here to greet you as well but she is..." He paused to cough violently once more.

"My lord you should rest." The beautiful woman put her hand at his elbow as his body was wracked with coughs. She must be the new Lady Fujimori then. Pity. Though he supposed he couldn't be too disappointed. If the real Yuki were half as beautiful as this woman, he'd have no qualms.

Hotaru bowed. "I look forward to meeting her."

Lord Fujimori frowned, not bothering to disguise his displeasure. He'd only just arrived and he was stepping on toes. But even if this man was a recent lord, he knew the dance. What other reason would an unmarried lord come than to make a marital alliance? Especially in times of war.

"You and your men must be tired—" Lord Fujimori said.

Someone shouted behind him, and Hotaru turned just as a woman collided with him, knocking him onto the ground. Hotaru looked up at the woman who straddled him. Her hair was frizzy and there was dirt smeared on her cheek. Despite her filthy appearance, she was rather pretty, with large eyes and a rosebud mouth.

She leaped off him without so much as a 'sorry' and hurried up the steps toward the young lord. No one moved to stop her. It was the same wild woman he'd seen in the forest. She bowed low to Lord Fujimori, her braid falling over her shoulder.

"I'm sorry, brother. I'll get washed up before our guests arrive."

Lord Fujimori sighed, before gesturing toward Hotaru. "Lord Kaedemori, I'd like to introduce you to my sister, Yuki."

2

Yuki stalked through the forest, breathing in and out methodically. The forest spoke to her, not so much in words, but in feelings and images. She knew each plant and animal by name. If she reached out she could touch their energy, and let her own commune with it. If she wanted to hunt deer, she could command it to come to her. If she were foraging, the forest would guide her to what she was looking for. But there was only one prey she had her mind on today. The soft earth cradled her bare feet as she crept through the shadows. The wind blew toward her, carrying her scent away from her target.

The tanuki had its back to her as it dug under a fallen log searching for grubs. Its long-striped tail wiggled back and forth. The chubby animal was completely unaware. Yuki raised her weapon over her head, poised for attack. Then the wind changed. The raccoon dog lifted its head, its black nose flaring and whiskers trembling. Before it was too late and it scurried away, Yuki launched herself at the animal, but the tanuki was faster and scurried into the underbrush before she could catch it.

Knocking the bush with her weapon, she scared it out of its hiding space and it bolted across the forest floor. She gave chase, following its zig-zagging trail through the forest. It darted into a nearby cave, one she could sense had no exit. There was no escaping now.

"I've got you now," she called in a sing-song voice.

Her voice echoed back at her, distorted and multiplied. It sounded as if she were surrounded. A chill ran up her spine as a cold spring wind blew through the mouth of the cave with a mournful howl. The cave stank of mold and brackish water. It dripped from an unknown source. The ground was slimy and her feet slid along looking for stable ground. She clutched her weapon close to her side as the small hairs on the back of her head rose up. She was being watched.

"I'm not going to hurt you. There's no need to hide," she said, trying to coax it out. Not that that tactic ever worked.

Yuki scanned the darkness, but the light from beyond could not penetrate deep within the belly of the cave and she squinted as she searched for the tanuki. Then one single yellow eye appeared. At first at her height and then rose higher and higher, towering over her. Yuki stumbled backward, clutching her weapon as a roar from the monster's mouth shook the ground beneath her feet. The yokai's razor-sharp teeth gleamed in the dark.

Yuki turned and ran, the monster close behind her. Its thundering footsteps echoed behind her. In her momentary wild panic, she stumbled and almost fell, but caught herself at the last moment. As she slowed down the oni should have caught up with her, but when she looked back he was no closer than before. She turned around to face the beast with her weapon drawn.

"You want to fight?"

The oni came up short, skidding to a stop just before her. Using her wooden stick, she struck the oni on top of the head. The creature exploded in a puff of smoke and seven tanuki tumbled onto the ground. Each wore a straw hat and different colored haori. When standing they all hardly came up to her hip. One of them had a lump on his head, and Yuki gave the other six matching lumps. They all fell to their knees, groveling for mercy.

Yuki looked down at them, hands on hips. "Did you really think I was going to fall for that?"

"We almost had you this time," said Happi.

"It was worth a try," said Kushami.

She squatted down beside them, so she was at their eye level. They were basically children, by yokai standards anyway. But they had told her once they were over a hundred years old. In many ways they acted just as human children would. And she treated them as such.

"Give it to me," she held out her hand. It had been two days of chasing them through the forest trying to get it back.

It was Shai who broke from the rank and handed her the necklace. She snatched it from his hand, and her finger traced over the pendant. Pale pink petals made of precious stone were set around a central stone. They couldn't have known how important it was to her when they stole it. Yuki put it back around her neck and then stood up, glaring at the tanuki.

"You have to promise me not to steal anymore." She waggled her finger at them.

"We promise!" they chirped in unison.

Yuki smiled. "Shall we play some more then?"

They leaped up, cheering for more, grabbing her arms and pulling her toward the forest to play.

"Didn't you have a dinner tonight?" said Kashikoi, the oldest of the tanuki and self-proclaimed leader.

Yuki rolled her eyes, she'd almost forgotten about the new arrival. From what she'd glimpsed of him, he was no different than the rest. "Oh yes, how could I forget."

She was in no hurry to get back. How many different men had come vying for her hand since her father's death? "We can play a little while and then I'll head back. I still have plenty of time." She rubbed Kashikoi's head and he leaned into her touch.

By the time they finished playing it was dark out. She had completely missed the welcome dinner for Lord-what's-his-face. Instead she went by the kitchens, begging for scraps. The head cook had a plate set aside and a lecture about how a proper young lady should act. Yuki endured it, shoveling food into her mouth. Yuki ate standing in the kitchen before going to beg her brother for forgiveness.

The lights were dim in his room, but she knew Riku wouldn't be asleep yet.

"Brother?" Yuki called from outside his bedroom door.

She waited for a response. When one did not come straight away she feared he was actually mad at her this time.

"Come in," came a rattling reply, followed by a cough.

Yuki frowned. His cough was getting worse. She crept into the room, head bowed. Riku was lying on his futon, eyes closed and taking slow, rattling breaths.

She knelt beside him. His health only seemed to be worsening. What started out as a slight cold and fever lingered and grew stronger over the passing weeks. He hardly ate, and mostly drank a special brew of tea. He was wasting away a little more every day. *Don't be ridiculous. It's just a lingering cold.* But what cold lasted for over a month and persisted despite the warming weather? She couldn't stand the thought it was happening again.

His cheeks were hollowed out and the circles under his eyes were getting darker. He was a skull with skin stretched over it. His hands were fragile and pale, much too pale. Yuki brushed his fevered forehead with the back of her hand. He should be resting, not entertaining some arrogant lord.

"We shouldn't have guests until you get better," Yuki scolded.

"I'm just tired, that's all. I'll be fine after I rest."

She held his hand, rubbing her thumb over the digits. That's what he had been saying for weeks, but he was only getting worse.

"Why waste your time? He's just like the rest."

Riku took another shaking breath. "I know."

"Why does it even matter to us? The forest will protect us, let them destroy one another."

He turned toward her, his eyes glassy. "I don't care about the war. But I do want to know you're taken care of when I'm gone."

Something took a hold of her stomach and twisted. "You're too young to worry about things like that."

He squeezed her hand, or at least he tried to. He'd gotten so weak. She couldn't hide her frown.

"It's time you married," he said.

"I will not marry without love you know that." She felt she needed to remind him. It was just an excuse really. There'd never been anyone who'd made her heart race. And she wasn't even sure that sort of thing was possible. Her father said he had loved her mother, and that when she'd died it had destroyed him. And yet he married again.

He patted her hand, "I know, my heart."

That had been her father's nickname for her. The heart of the household. Her father's death was too fresh. It hadn't been a full season since he died. She couldn't get married now, not when Riku was sick. Besides, this was where she belonged and this is where she would stay.

"What do you think he wants?" Yuki asked her brother as she tucked him in like a baby.

"You, most likely."

Yuki's hands froze. "He hasn't asked you yet? How tactful," she said as she smoothed the blankets over him.

"I was hoping to introduce you at dinner tonight," her brother said, with the ghost of the smile she remembered on his face.

"I lost track of time while I was in the forest."

"Maybe if you could just talk to him—"

"To what end?"

"Whether we like it or not, war is coming, and we're going to have to pick a side," he said, and tried to be authoritative but he went into a coughing fit instead. His entire body shook with it and each time, Yuki felt as if she were being stabbed in the gut.

"Then why don't you marry, brother? You're the clan leader, you need an heir," she said, trying to lighten the mood.

He clutched his bedding as he continued to cough. Eventually the coughing subsided and he looked at her, his eyes bloodshot.

"Listen to me, Yuki. I'm not getting any better. If I cannot produce an heir in time, then it will be your son who takes over the clan. I've already decided."

"You'll find a wife soon enough." She couldn't stand this kind of talk. He sounded like her father at the end. She refused to believe he was dying.

"Promise me, Yuki."

She swallowed past a lump in her throat. "I promise. But only if you promise to live a very long life."

They stared at one another, already she could see a dark shadow creeping around his aura. The same she'd seen before their father died. They thought it an illness, but no one had gotten sick but her brother and her father, one after the other. The people in the clan whispered about a curse, but she didn't want to believe. He had to live. He just had to.

3

"Yuki?" The man scratched his chin as he stared at the sky. "She's a good girl, more or less."

There was something he wasn't saying and he was too quick to return to cleaning. His attention was focused on wringing out a rag into a bucket. The hallway behind him sparkled and was in no need of cleaning. But he continued to fiddle with it, wiping the same spot over and over.

The clan was strange. No matter who he asked, he heard the same thing. He'd be lying to say he wasn't intrigued. There was something wild and untamed about her and this place. The Fujimoris were in a position of strategic importance: their territory, placed as it was in between him and the Fujikawa's and filled with thick forest, could help him gain the advantage in the war. In addition to that, they were said to be fierce fighters.

"Isn't she a bit...wild?" Hotaru asked.

"She spends a fair bit of time in the forest." He shrugged and picked up his bucket, perhaps deciding he was only going to avoid this conversation by walking away.

Hotaru followed after him, taking the burden of the bucket from him. "Is that typical of your clan?"

The old man laughed, nervously. He kept eyeing the bucket and then scanning the hallway. "Oh, no, Yuki, is eh... unique in that way."

The water sloshed around in the bucket threatening to soak the front of his clothes as he followed the servant down the hall. Apart from running into one another briefly upon his arrival, he hadn't seen a sign of her. And he had looked.

"Does she always run around barefoot and chase animals?" Hotaru asked.

"A bit." They arrived at a courtyard and the servant reached for the bucket, but Hotaru held it outside his reach.

"Why is she like that? Is there something wrong with her?"

The servant sighed, realizing there was no way of avoiding his questions. "She didn't have a mother to teach her how to be a lady. And the former Lord Fujimori would take her into the woods, taught her to fight and hunt. It's no wonder she chased away the others." He mumbled the last under his breath.

"The others?" Hotaru prompted, finally getting to the heart of things.

The servant, realizing he had said too much, cleared his throat. "Why are you asking these questions?"

"Just curious, you could say," Hotaru replied as he handed the bucket back to the servant.

"Curious about what exactly?" said a woman from behind him.

Hotaru plastered a charming smile on his face and turned to see Yuki glaring at him with hands on her hips. She'd recently re-braided her hair and washed the dirt from her face. Without the dirty smudges and tangled hair, she was actually beautiful. The rumors had only been a slight exaggeration then. But her clothing confirmed what the servant had said, she wore a plain hakama and haori, close fitted and similar to what he wore when he was sparring. Not something he would have expected of a young lady. But he was coming to realize there was nothing predictable about her.

"I wanted to learn more about you."

She smiled sweetly, but it didn't quite reach her eyes. "Oh really?"

"I was hoping we could be formally introduced. I am Lord Kaedemori, but you can call me Hotaru." He bowed to her, deeply, giving her the utmost respect. She gave him a quick shallow bow.

"I heard you've been asking about me." She took a step closer toward him.

I hoped she would. Nothing lured a woman in like knowing a man was interested. "I wanted to get to know you. In times like these it's good for us to work together. Make new bonds." He inched closer to her.

"The way I heard it, the Kaedemoris and the Fujikawas were working together."

"You're very informed, for a woman." Could she know about the falling out between his clan and the Fujikawas?

She'd gotten very close now, where he could smell a faint flowery scent, perhaps her bath water. Her lashes were long and framed large brown eyes. "Are you saying because I'm a woman, I shouldn't be informed?"

"It is unusual for a woman to know about the dealings between the clans."

The fake sweet smile was wiped from her face. "Or perhaps I should be sitting quietly in the corner, like a delicate decoration, ready to be traded in an alliance?"

Her response had caught him off guard. It was the first time a woman had disarmed him with just her words. She fluttered her eyelashes at him, waiting for a response.

"Not at all," he stammered

"Then why are you asking about my family and me like one would livestock?" The intensity of her glare was enough to set him on fire.

"I'm sorry. I believe I've offended you somehow." He bowed to her, hoping to salvage the situation.

She laughed. "You don't even know what you've done wrong?"

"Perhaps if you could explain it to me?" He smiled in a way that made other girls swoon. But it only seemed to make her angrier.

She curled her hands into fists at her side and her face was flushed. It was rather charming. She was even more spirited than he had thought.

"Why did you come here, really?" she said through gritted teeth.

It seemed crude to bring up a marital alliance before he had a chance to speak with her brother. It would be his decision after all. And so he said, "I believe that's between your brother and I."

"Is that so?"

She marched over to the servant who'd been watching their exchange and grabbed the bucket from his hands. Then she stomped over to Hotaru and dumped the contents of the bucket over his head, dousing him in cold water. He gasped and sputtered, shaking the water from his hands and wiping it off his face.

"What was that for?"

She pointed her finger at him. "Hear this now: I'm not interested in marrying you or anyone."

He glared after her. *What did I do wrong?* He'd always been good with women, able to charm any woman. But it was becoming clear, Yuki wasn't like most women.

4
_____

Yuki sat in the round window of her room that looked at the forest beyond. She should be out there. Suimin, the tanuki, dozed in her lap as she stroked his fur. The moon was full in the sky and cast a pale light over the garden. She could feel spring trembling beneath the surface of the sleeping forest. She wanted to be out there, to watch the flowers bloom, feel the forest awaken again.

Instead she was trapped by the promise she'd made to Riku, caged behind the walls of the palace. One of her legs dangled out her window, her back leaning against the frame. She told her brother she'd give this new suitor a chance. And she was going to this time, she really was. She'd even gone looking for him this afternoon. But he was more insufferable than all the ones who'd come before him. How arrogant. How repulsive. She scrunched her nose up in disgust.

There was a knock at the door. The other six tanuki who were playing in her room froze, taking the shape of items around her room. Kashikoi a book, Happi a brazier in the corner, and so on. Suimin hardly cracked an eye open before flopping onto her futon and pretending to be a pillow, one with a suspicious striped tail. She hid his tail beneath the blanket before going to answer.

The maid peered into the room. "Are you ready for dinner?"

Yuki, still in her same clothes from that afternoon, shrugged. "Just about." She looked to the open window. It wouldn't be hard to climb out the window and then over the far wall. She did it all the time.

"Lord Fujimori told me to remind you of your promise," the maid said, knowing as everyone in the palace did, that she was not easily confined indoors.

Yuki sighed heavily. She had promised, hadn't she?

"I'll only be a few more minutes."

The maid looked skeptical as she bowed her head and closed the door. Yuki turned back to the tanuki. Most of them had resumed their normal forms. She said she would come, but she hadn't promised she'd behave.

"How would you guys like to have a little fun tonight?" she asked.

The seven voices cheered with excitement.

Yuki dressed and headed to dinner. She had to suppress her smile or Riku would be suspicious. The entire clan had gathered in the dining room. Everyone was eager to catch a glimpse of the handsome stranger. Their territory was so isolated they rarely saw outsiders. Riku sat at the head of the room, her spot beside him empty, and that man was seated on the other side of the empty space. This was Riku's plan to force them together, just as he'd done with all the others. For once, she was glad he had.

Her stepmother was seated to the other side of her brother. She saw Yuki enter and smiled and waved at her. Yuki ignored her as she made her way through the crowd. Even after her father's death her stepmother remained, and acted as caretaker to her brother. She'd been married to her father less than a year when he'd passed. And being just a few years older than Yuki, she could never see her as a mother.

As Yuki made her way to her seat, the clan members muttered to themselves.

"How long will this one last?"

"I heard she poured water over his head."

"Who would take such a girl as a bride?"

She forced a smile and kept walking, ignoring their criticisms. Each step she took she felt Hotaru's eyes on her. She had hoped she'd made her decision clear. Normally she didn't need to take such drastic measures. Most of the suitors had left not long after arriving, thinking she was a feral beast. She wasn't wife material, she needed her freedom to roam. She couldn't be a painted doll locked in a room all day. She'd go mad.

But either he was exceedingly stubborn, or very stupid. She'd like to think it was the latter of the two. She'd taken the long way to her seat, hoping to delay the inevitable. But as she got closer she gave him a shallow bow, and their eyes met. He was handsome, she'd give him that. But the handsome veneer couldn't take away the rotten core underneath. She sat down next to him, keeping as much space between them as possible.

"You look lovely," he said.

She snorted in disbelief. *How original.*

Riku gave her a discreet pinch. Yuki hissed, to keep from crying out. She glared at her brother and was prepared to return the pinch with a punch, but seeing his frail body, she hesitated. He gave her a look that said, 'you promised.'

Yuki plastered on a fake smile and turned toward Lord Kaedemori. "Would you like a drink?"

She held up a jug of sake.

He held out his cup for her to fill. While she concentrated on pouring he continued to stare. It was a bit disconcerting, feeling his eyes upon her. It made her stomach squirm unpleasantly. She glanced up at him, wondering what it was about her face that was so interesting. Up close, and without his mouth moving, he was very handsome. The ghost of stubble over his chin and his smile were very alluring. Distracted, she overfilled his cup and liquor spilled onto his haori. He jerked backward, spilling the glass and all of its contents onto the ground.

"Oh, I'm so sorry," she said with a complete lack of sincerity.

He kept that same charming smile in place as he wiped it away. "No matter, it was me who was a bit clumsy."

She forced a laugh and then looked away, letting her smile drop. She scanned the room until she spotted a servant carrying in the first course. He knelt down to give a plate to one of her cousins and she noticed the striped tail sticking out from beneath his haori.

Yuki stifled her laughter behind her hand and covered it with a cough.

"I wanted to apologize for what I said this afternoon," he said.

Yuki turned toward him, eyebrows raised. "Oh really?"

"I've heard a lot about your beauty, and they say you're a very intriguing woman."

She had to resist the urge to roll her eyes. So he hadn't really learned his lesson. It was all just lip service.

"I got tongue-tied in front of you, and I said some things I didn't mean," he said as he leaned toward her.

It took all of her willpower to not flee from the room. Her only saving grace was Baka, disguised as a servant and carrying a bowl that was teetering dangerously close to the edge of the tray.

"Uh huh," she choked out as she tried to contain her laughter.

"You see—" Before he could finish his sentence, the bowl of soup Baka was carrying tipped over onto the lord's lap.

The puffed-up lord gasped in surprise, and Yuki waited for him to explode in anger.

"Oh my lord, I am so sorry," Baka said as he attempted to clean up the spill.

"No, it's fine really," Hotaru replied, bending down at the same time Baka stood up.

The top of Baka's head struck Hotaru in the nose. Unprepared for the collision, Baka's illusionary magic faltered. And fearing she'd be caught, Yuki leaped up, putting herself in between Hotaru and Baka, whose ears and tail were already showing. But Baka was also trying to get away and instead knocked Yuki into Hotaru. He caught her and she stared up at him, shocked and frozen. There was a small trickle of blood coming from his nose.

"Oh sir, you're bleeding," said Kushami, another tanuki disguised as a servant.

Yuki leaped away from him, Baka had made his escape, and she was no longer needed to make a diversion. Kushami was attempting to wipe away the blood from Hotaru's face but had to sneeze mid-way through and accidentally swiped blood across his face.

"I'm fine, really," Hotaru said in exasperation, taking the cloth from Kushami.

But Kushami wouldn't let go and what resulted was a tug of war, each of them refusing to give up the bloody rag.

"That's enough!" her brother said.

The tanuki bowed as he dropped the cloth, leaving Hotaru with his bloody trophy. The tanuki backed away, and Yuki gave him a wink. Hotaru was brought more soup, and dinner continued on as normal. When the meal was finished, Hotaru stood up.

"I have brought gifts," he said and gestured to the far end of the room. His soldiers carried in three chests. It took two men to carry a single chest. The clansmen mumbled their approval, speculating as to what could be inside. Lord Kaedemori had brought more than his predecessors, that was for sure. All the suitors brought presents. It was the price for buying a bride after all.

But when the first chest was opened, a foul smell filled the room. Everyone gagged and covered their mouths and noses.

"What is that?" Yuki cried, knowing perfectly well what it was. It had been her idea after all.

"It looks to be filled with rotting fish heads." Her brother coughed and her stepmother handed him a handkerchief to help him cover his mouth.

Hotaru leaped up slammed the chest shut. "Take this away," he growled at his men, then to Riku he said, "I am so sorry, my lord, I don't know what happened. That was not the chest I brought."

"It looks like your chest," Yuki said, smiling. Hotaru was scratching his head.

From the corner of her eye, she felt Riku watching her. A second chest was brought out and this one was filled with human bones and skulls and what looked to be grave soil. One woman screamed and several others made the sign of warding.

"Why would you bring a curse into our house?" Yuki asked.

Hotaru walked over to the chest and stared down at it. "I swear this is not what I brought. It should be filled with silk..."

"Perhaps we should save the gifts for later," Riku said with another stern look her in direction.

She only smiled sweetly back at him.

The young lord came back to sit, shaking his head. As he did he passed by one of the rooms braziers and an unseen tanuki grabbed his sleeve and brought it to the flame. The sleeve caught, spreading quickly. It took only a few moments for him to realize what was happening.

Another of the tanuki in disguise suggested he roll onto the ground. Hotaru fell onto the ground and rolled vigorously. While Yuki, ready with a jug of water, leaped up and poured more of it over his face than onto the sleeve.

She gave a fake sheepish smile. "Oh, I'm sorry. I didn't mean to get you all wet... again."

The lord looked at her, suspicion in his gaze. But he couldn't really blame her. He'd been on fire, was she supposed to just let him burn?

"I'm fortunate you are so quick on your feet," he said as he shook off his wet clothes. He smirked at her, as if he knew she'd been behind all the evening's misfortunes. But how could he accuse her? None of the others had ever suspected.

"Perhaps now is a good time to end this night's... entertainment," Riku said with a look in Yuki's direction. He knew it was her, and she would get an earful later. But it was worth it to see the backside of Lord Kaedemori.

The lord looked down at his soaked clothes and shrugged. "A few wet clothes don't bother me much."

He smirked at her again. It was a challenge. He was not going to be as easy to get rid of as the others.

5

She poured tea gracefully, her eyes lowered. She gave him a demure glance, as to not meet his eye. Hotaru tried not to look in her direction but she was beautiful. Dark hair, pale skin, long lashes, and ruby red lips.

Lord Fujimori took the tea and brought it to his lips.

"We are honored to have you here, cousin. I am sorry it is under such sad circumstances." The young lord was not that far apart in age from Hotaru. But due to his diminished size, he looked like a boy. The new Lord Fujimori was frail as rice paper, and looked ready to keel over at any moment. If rumors were true, the family was desperate for an alliance and Hotaru was not the first to come looking for one. It didn't matter what Hotaru wanted, though. It was what they needed.

"I am sorry I did not get the chance to meet your father. My father spoke very highly of him," Hotaru lied.

In fact, Hotaru's father never spoke highly of anyone. Getting praise from him was like trying to get blood from a turnip. Not going to happen. But he figured a few kind lies wouldn't hurt negotiations.

The Lady Fujimori sat at the back of the room with her eyes

lowered. His gaze was drawn to her. Why bring his wife to these negotiations? Then again, from what he had seen so far, the Fujimori women were a very different breed.

"Your father was well known to us as well. It is a pity we both lost them too soon and now the burden of running the clans falls to us." He pressed his sleeve to his lips to cover his cough. His skin was near translucent, and the dark circles under his eyes made him look as if he hadn't slept in ages. *Hikaru would know what to say in this situation. He was always better with words than me.* But his brother wasn't clan leader, he was.

"We're fortunate we have families that support us," Hotaru said.

"Let us not dance around the subject. Why have you come here?"

This frail lord didn't look it, but he was shrewd. And Hotaru felt out of his depth. He was no diplomat. He was better with a sword. If only women did run the clans, he'd have no problem getting what he wanted. *Unless it was Yuki.* Just thinking of the previous night and her sly smirk, there was not a doubt in his mind who had switched the chests. But how had she done it? They'd been guarded from the moment he arrived. Hotaru pushed it from his mind.

"As you know, there has been fighting between the clans lately. Our families share a common ancestry and I came to extend an offer of alliance through marriage."

"What can you offer us?" Lord Fujimori asked.

The young lord looked at him with gray eyes, all color looked as if it had seeped out of him, like the rest of his pale skin. This man would not last until summer and running an entire clan in this condition must be extremely taxing. He would be doing them a favor by marrying his sister. It would strengthen their clan to be united with a wealthy and powerful clan like the Kaedemoris. If he were to have an heir before he died, Hotaru could guard that

child's seat. Though given the state he was in, Hotaru doubted
he'd have a child in time.

But he wouldn't say all that. He'd already had too many
missteps since he'd arrived.

"We can offer you protection," Hotaru replied.

"The forest protects us."

The forest, though historically a place of refuge, couldn't
protect them from the Fujikawas. They were out for blood, and
no one would be safe while Lord Fujikawa was on a rampage. He
wanted to conquer the entire region, maybe the entire island.

"It cannot protect you in this case," Hotaru replied.

"What makes you so sure?" Lady Fujimori spoke up.

At first Hotaru was speechless. It was one thing to allow her to
stay during these proceedings, but for her to speak? That was
unheard of. He stared at her for a moment, mouth agape. She
lowered her eyes, realizing her mistake, and her husband spoke in
her stead.

"What makes you think the forest will not protect us when it
has done so since the dawn of time?" He made no excuse for his
wife, which in itself was strange, but Hotaru ignored it.

"Because the Fujikawas are strong, and they do not fear the
forest. They've already made alliances with many other clans, and
rumor has it you rejected their proposal. Lord Fujimori does not
forgive or forget. Once his army has conquered the other territo-
ries, he will come for you next."

"Do you know what this forest is? It is not just wood and
plants. It is alive," Lord Fujimori said in a hushed tone.

Hotaru had seen only a hint of the world of yokai and the
kami. Their influence had changed the trajectory of his family and
he did not doubt the power of this place. It was part of the reason
he'd come here but even magic wasn't enough to stop the
coming war.

"Do you hope the goodwill of the kami will protect you? What
will you do when they come with axes and fire?"

"You cannot understand the pacts we have made, the sacrifices..." he trailed off.

So it wasn't just a rumor.

"I am glad the forest will protect you, but can it save your livelihood? The food you need to survive, if the Fujikawas cut off your trade routes, then what? How will you feed your people?"

"We are not the ones who started this war, Lord Kaedemori," he said quietly.

He'd pinned him. Hotaru fumbled to find the right thing to say. But he feared anything he could say would make him look like a desperate fool. He'd been so desperate to rule, but he'd never known what it really meant. When Hikaru stepped down, Hotaru had inherited a war and a mess he was left to untangle. All he had left was the truth.

"I know your health is failing. I can secure your descendant's rule and I will protect your wife once you pass." He nodded toward the woman behind him.

"I am unmarried. This woman is my father's second wife. She provided my father counsel before his death, and so she does me."

Hotaru looked at the young, beautiful woman. She could not be much older than himself. To think of her married to someone that had to have been his own father's age seemed a crime. And stranger yet, this young lord took counsel from his stepmother? What a strange family indeed.

"You speak of marital alliance but your brother's marriage to Lady Fujikawa was the start of this mess. "

Hotaru kept his expression neutral, though he was boiling on the inside. He knew word would get out. He could not hide it forever but the choices his brother had made were his own. Hikaru had given up his role as an elder, and left everything behind for love.

"Our alliance with the Fujikawas ran into complications. Lady Fujikawa ran away with a lover, but her family believes that she died while in our care. Without evidence otherwise war was inevitable, unfortunately."

Lord Fujimori nodded his head. "My sister's child will be my heir. You understand, this is not a decision I can make lightly."

Hotaru bowed his head. "I understand completely. What can I do to help you make a decision?"

Just then the doors to the room were slid open. Yuki, her face flushed, stormed in.

"Yuki," Lady Fujimori stood up, and motioned to intervene. Yuki pushed past her as if she weren't there at all and placed herself between Hotaru and her brother, with her back to him.

"You promised me!" she said.

"Yuki, now is not the time for this." Lord Fujimori held up his hands, trying to calm her.

"You told me it was my choice!"

"We will talk later."

"Yuki, come with me." Her stepmother grabbed her by the arm but Yuki shook her off, accidentally slapping her across the face.

Her stepmother touched her cheek, tears welling up in her eyes.

"What did you do?" her brother snapped, rushing to his stepmother's side, grabbing her by shoulders. "Are you alright?" he asked her.

She nodded her head and turned away to wipe her tears.

"I refuse. Not him, brother, anyone but him." Yuki pointed at Hotaru, acknowledging his presence for the first time.

"Apologize to our mother," Lord Fujimori said.

"She is not my mother," Yuki snarled.

"Go." Lord Fujimori pointed to the door, and she stomped out, not before glaring at Hotaru as if this was all his fault. He watched her go, not certain if he should be concerned or impressed. There was a fire about her that drew him. But get too close and he might get burned.

6

The candle had burned low, and Riku had to squint to read the lines written on the parchment. His eyes grew tired more easily as of late. But he was determined to do his best for the clan while he still had time. The door to his room opened and he glanced up. His stepmother stood in the doorway, beautiful as ever. Her porcelain skin was marred by Yuki's slap. If only Yuki could see how kind their stepmother was, how desperately she wanted to take care of them. Now that their father was gone, she was all he had left to guide him. And perhaps she could teach Yuki how to be a proper lady as well.

"I won't be needing you tonight." He shifted papers between his hands, and his hands shook as he did so. Even these small tasks were growing too difficult to handle. If it wasn't for his stepmother, he didn't know how he could manage. He wanted everyone to believe that he was stronger than he was. But only she knew the true depths of his weakness. Even Yuki did not know. And hopefully she'd never find out.

But he couldn't ask her to tend to him after the scene Yuki had made. She must be mortified. With her delicate skin, that mark might even leave a bruise. She ignored his comments and came to sit close to him. Their knees brushed against one another and he tensed up. He pretended she wasn't sitting much too close to him and wrote something on the document in front of him. She touched his arm and he jerked back. His hand knocked into his ink block and splattered dark droplets onto the paper. They faded as they were absorbed by the fresh paper.

"You're so jumpy. I was only trying to move your ink block before you made a mess and now see what has happened."

His breath hitched. She cleaned up the mess, removed the stained paper, and re-wet his brush, handing it back to him. "There. Better?"

He nodded in agreement but he did not lift his pen again. His face was screwed up in concentration. She knew what was coming next.

"We cannot continue this. It's not right..."

She brushed her fingertips against his, one by one in a slow caress.

"You say different when I am wrapped around you."

He stood abruptly and paced to the opposite end of the room. Even that took a monumental effort. He ran his thin fingers through his hair and chunks came out in clumps. It was getting worse. All the same symptoms he'd witnessed in his father. Now it was happening to him. He stared at his hands in horror.

"I thought I had more time. It took my father almost a year before he was this bad." For Riku it had been less than three months.

She did not respond, but ran her hands along his back, her fingers gliding over the bumps along his spine, even with layers of fabric in between.

"You're working too hard," she purred in her ear. "Let me help you."

She slid around to the front, caressing his chest and moving downward. He gasped and put his hand on her shoulder. She looked at him from beneath her lashes.

"Go ahead, tell me to stop."

His eyes were fever-bright, conflicted and hungry. As much as he tried to pretend otherwise, he desired her: as insane, unhealthy, and forbidden as it was. He wanted her. His father's wife. His father's widow. She'd been too close in age to him to ever consider her a mother, but that was how the clan saw her. Stepmother. Mother. It made no difference. Their love was forbidden. But could they really call this perverse thing they were doing love?

She reached down his hakama. He groaned as she leaned forward and kissed his neck. Then she pulled back slightly. "We need Lord Kaedemori."

He shook his head. "Yuki won't have him."

She cupped his cheek. "It is your decision. You are a lord. Force her to marry him."

"I can't do that to her." He tried to turn away but she held on tight and he had become so weak.

But she knew how to play him as no one could. She pulled him toward the futon. He could try and fight her, but in the end, she always got what she wanted.

7

There was a key to every woman's heart. And Hotaru was determined to find Yuki's. The first obstacle was finding her. For such a small place it was well built for hiding. Asking the clan members was completely unhelpful. Most of them shrugged and others ignored him entirely.

After searching every possible inch of the palace, he was about to give up when he stumbled across the beautiful Lady Fujimori seated beneath the barren branches of a tree in a cold winter garden. Her bright kimono was like the first bloom of spring. Her gaze was fixed upon a pool at her feet where koi fish swam in circles, their mouths occasionally breaching the surface like tiny caves.

She must have felt him staring, because she glanced up at him. When their eyes met, she blushed and looked away. Being that she was a widow of the former clan leader, it would have been wiser not to flirt. But he was a sucker for a pretty face.

"I'm sorry to bother you," he said, cautiously.

She looked at him shyly, long eyelashes framing her wide round eyes. "It's no trouble. I was just feeding the fish. Care to join me?"

Unable to resist the request of a beautiful woman, he sat down beside her. "I can stay for a little while." He gave her his most charming smile.

"How have you enjoyed your stay here?" she asked as she gently tossed crumbs into the water for the fish. Even the flick of her wrist was graceful and controlled. She was the complete opposite of her wild stepdaughter. Her long pale fingers reached into the sack which held the feed. He could just imagine those hands caressing his body, reaching downward.

"Lord Kaedemori?" She tilted her head to the side as she peered at him.

Hotaru cleared his throat, realizing how rude he was being. "I've enjoyed it very much. There are so many beautiful sights here."

"I must admit your arrival here has been a breath of fresh air."

He met her gaze. Her eyes were dark, bottomless pools, so deep he felt he could drown in them. When he looked at her everything else melted away—he even forgot his own name. Why had he come here? All he knew was he desperately needed the woman who sat in front of him. Her ruby lips were parted ever so slightly, and he found himself consumed with the desire to press his lips against hers. He leaned in.

"What are you doing?" Yuki's accusatory tone yanked him back into the present. Hotaru stood up and spun toward Yuki who was standing at the edge of the garden, hands placed on her hips as she glared at the pair of them. He hadn't done anything wrong. They'd just been talking. And yet he felt as if he'd been caught by his jealous lover.

"I was—Uh." He looked back at Lady Fujimori, whose blush was more damning than words.

Hotaru could almost see flames in Yuki's stare. The heat of her anger could burn a hole through his forehead. He needed to explain.

He smiled and strode toward Yuki. "I was looking for you, Lady Yuki."

"Is that what you call flirting?" She scoffed and turned to walk away.

Damn it, he thought before he gave the Lady Fujimori a quick bow of his head. "I should be going, please excuse me." And chased after Yuki before giving his reply.

"I feel like you have the wrong impression of me," he said when he caught up with her.

"Ha!" she said keeping her head turned away from him no matter how he tried to catch her eye.

He jogged in front of her, throwing his arms out to stop her in her path. "Let's start over. I am Lord Kaedemori, but you can call me Hotaru." He gave her a formal bow, and finished it off with a charming grin.

She stared back at him, arms crossed over her chest. "Do you really think that's going to work?"

His smile broadened. "It's worked before."

She raised a single eyebrow. "You're rather experienced."

He chuckled. "There may be a few broken hearts in my past."

Her frown only deepened. It wasn't an encouraging sign. "And yet you've come here looking for a wife?"

"Your beauty is famed across the region. I could not pass up the opportunity to meet you. And perhaps more..." He waggled his eyebrows at her.

"The beauty of a wife is an important attribute?" She lowered her arms to her side and he took his chance to move closer to her. No woman could resist a compliment. She was just jealous of her stepmother. He'd seen that already. Well it seemed it was working in his favor.

He inched closer to her, and she tilted her head up to meet his gaze. "It is something I am looking for, yes."

She flushed from his compliment, and looked away shyly. "And what would not be desired?"

"I do like a strong-willed woman." He stepped closer to her and she backed up until her back was against the wall. He braced himself against it, leaning in close. Her entire face was flaming red now; he could feel the heat radiating off of her. "Someone like you."

She bit her lip, pulling his eyes toward it. Was she teasing him, trying to drive him mad? Perhaps all her obstinance had just been for show. "And what do you think of a woman who speaks her mind?" Her eyes fluttered up to him.

He leaned closer to whisper in her ear, "I like it when they speak their desires... in the bedchamber. "

She looked up, meeting his gaze at last. "You're going to be very disappointed then."

"Why is that?"

She lurched forward, slamming her shoulder into his chest. It caught him by surprise and before he had time to react, she grabbed a hold of his arm and flipped him over her head. He landed hard on his back, the air forced from his lungs. As he lay gasping for breath, she leaned over him.

"Because you'll never see me in your bedchamber."

As he lay gasping, utterly humiliated, he realized she had been playing him the entire time. Before he could recover, she scurried away and out of reach. Hotaru was never the type to turn down a challenge. Yuki wasn't a woman, but a beast in disguise.

Hotaru returned to his room and kicked over the box of gifts he'd brought with him. It did little to assuage his frustration and instead resulted in a stubbed toe. He hissed under his breath as he examined the throbbing digit.

The contents of the chest spilled out onto the ground. A jeweled comb, a very expensive silk kimono. He'd chose them with the intention of wooing Yuki. What woman didn't like shiny trinkets? But somehow even that had been ruined. He hadn't figured out how Yuki had turned the treasure into bones, or the silks into rotting fish heads. When he had gone to investigate after the dinner they'd all returned to normal. Taking out his anger on the useless hunks of metal and cloth, he threw them across the room. A jade hairpin hit the far wall, snapping in half.

I don't have time to waste on that woman. Hotaru picked up a yellow kimono with a pattern of red and blue flowers. He was about to rend it in two when the soft tinkle of bells froze him in place.

"It would seem things are not going as planned," said a raspy voice.

Hotaru dropped the kimono, which pooled at his feet. He put a smile on his face and turned to his uninvited guest. "What a pleasant surprise. I did not think I would see you here."

The witch smiled, deepening the grooves in her face, turning her skin into a garish mask. Her smile always made him uneasy. "I came to check on your progress." She stooped down to pick up the comb off the ground. "I thought you could win any woman. But it seems Lady Yuki is more difficult than you expected."

"Why her? There are plenty of other clans with greater armies."

The witch rolled the comb around in her hand without looking up at him. "The Fujimoris are different. You could not understand. If you want to win your war, you need them."

"Why must you speak in the riddles? What can they do to win me this war?"

The witch waggled her finger in front of him. "Time is running out. Lord Kaedemori has won many of your neighbors against you." She marched over to him and placed the comb in his hand. "Don't lose sight, win the girl and the alliance and you'll have everything you wanted."

Hotaru's hand clenched the comb. He had no other choice, he must win Yuki over.

8

As a peace offering, Hotaru had sent Yuki the comb. It was one of the few gifts that remained intact. Since he was certain she wouldn't accept it directly from him, he sent it with a maid and a note apologizing, again, for the way he acted. Though he didn't see what he'd done wrong. Women liked apologies.

When he arrived in the dining hall that night Yuki was already seated beside her brother. Even from across the way, her smile lit up the room and the sickly Lord Fujimori looked almost animated as they talked.

Yuki was a bit rough around the edges, her clothes were plain, and even indoors there was a wild energy to her. Her face was flushed and full of life, and her long, ebony hair had been pulled back with the comb he had sent. He had half expected her to reject his gift. She turned as he came into the room, and there was a genuine smile on her face. *Perhaps I am making progress after all.*

Seeing that gave him the confidence he needed and he strolled in to join his hosts.

"Good evening, Lord Fujimori, Lady Yuki." Yuki's vibrant energy was even more intoxicating up close. It was easy to forget she'd flipped him earlier that day. It was like he was looking at a different girl entirely. He couldn't stop staring. *Was this another trick?*

She must have felt his stare, because Yuki bit her lip and turned away from him. Then almost too quiet to hear she said, "Thank you for the gift, it's lovely."

Now he was certain this was a trick. There was no way she'd changed that much since the afternoon. He decided to play along.

"It looks even better on you than I could have imagined."

Throughout dinner he chatted with the clansmen, avoiding engaging Yuki in conversation. He would make her come to him. If she were trying to deceive him as he suspected, it wouldn't be long.

Though he made an effort to avoid her, his eyes were continually drawn to Yuki. Every time before she'd seemed like a feral animal, but tonight she was a blooming flower. Though he never engaged with her in conversation, when he told a bad joke to one of the clansmen she laughed at it and he swore he'd heard her snort. But when he glanced in her direction, she had turned crimson and kept her face away from him.

Could he be breaking down her walls, or was she that good at pretending? Or perhaps it was the comb. The witch had been fiddling with it. She must have put a spell on it. The idea of wooing a woman with something other than his own charm didn't sit right with him. He decided to test the theory.

Halfway through dinner he leaned over to her, his lips inches from her ear. And she leaned toward him. The moment was surprisingly intimate, and he half expected her to slap him for daring to get this close.

"Join me in the garden after dinner?" he asked.

"I would love to," she replied with a secretive smile.

It seemed naive to do so, but his heart raced a bit at the prospect.

After dinner, Hotaru made a show of going back to his room. The reasonable part of him knew she'd likely not show up and make a fool of him, or worse she'd set him up for an even greater embarrassment he couldn't imagine. But when he arrived at the moonlit garden, she was there waiting for him. The palace did not have the same sort of cultivated gardens of his own home. These were much more untamed: dead vines grew over walls and yellow grass grew in thick clumps between stepping stones. The pathways meandered through dense foliage. In the middle of spring he imagined it would be green and lush, but at the edges of winter, it was a dreary landscape. Not the romantic rendezvous he would have imagined.

To his surprise Yuki was waiting for him beneath the outstretched branches of a tree, staring up at the nearly full moon. In the moonlight, she looked like a goddess. As if she were the goddess of the moon come down from the heavens, she seemed to glow with ethereal light. Insects chirped and night birds sang as they hunted.

"Are you really here, or is this a manifestation of my dreams?" Hotaru asked.

She turned to him, eyes wide and lips parted ever so slightly. "Oh, you startled me."

He took a step closer, but was almost afraid to get too close. As if there were an invisible boundary that once he crossed, it would startle her and she would flee into the woods like a scared rabbit.

"I apologize, I didn't mean to. I just thought after this afternoon you wanted nothing to do with me." He hadn't meant to be quite so honest. But there was a strange, vulnerable innocence to her expression. She really hadn't noticed him staring. He cleared his throat and looked at the moon. "What were you looking at?"

"The first sign of spring." She gestured to the tree branch and a single bud on the tip of the branch. "The peach tree blooms first, then fruit comes in the summer."

She toyed with a necklace around her throat. It appeared to be a flower made of precious stones.

"Is this your favorite tree?" he asked.

She looked back at him, the magic was gone and her expression closed, leaving him with the girl he'd come to know.

"It was my mother's. My father planted it for her when they wed." She turned her back on the tree. "Why did you ask me to come here?"

"I thought we could stroll by the moonlight." He gave her a lazy grin.

She chuckled. "I have to give you credit. You're much more persistent. The other suitors would have run away by now."

"But I'm different."

"Oh?" She raised an eyebrow in question.

"Let me guess, they all start out the same: with kind words and pretty gifts, but none of them really see the real you."

She watched him warily. "And who is the real me?"

"Someone who loves her independence."

The question seemed to startle her, and she blinked at him for a moment before turning away. He'd hit the nail on the head, he was certain of it.

Her reply was so quiet it was unintelligible and he leaned in closer to hear.

"What was that?" he asked.

In reply there was a loud raspberry sound. As if he had passed wind. Hotaru froze in place, his eyes scanning around him. They were having a moment and now she was going to think he was passing gas?

He cleared his throat.

"You—" but before he could form a sentence, he heard it again. "Did you hear that?" he asked.

"Hear what?" she said, with what sounded like a hardly suppressed giggle.

He'd been a fool to think she was really opening up to him. In a rage, he grabbed her by the shoulder, spinning her around to face him.

"This may be a game to you, but it isn't to me. I came here with sincere intentions—" Once more his speech was cut off by a loud, offensive noise.

Yuki looked up at him, fluttering her eyelashes innocently. But if it wasn't her, then who'd made that sound?

"What is it?" she asked coyly.

"I know this is your doing. Just like I know it was you who replaced my gifts with fish heads."

"How could I?"

"It was yokai magic," he said, and was satisfied to see the shock register on her face. At last he'd pinned her.

That was why the witch had insisted he make an alliance with the Fujimoris. They had the yokai on their side. And if they could convince them to play petty tricks, what more could they do? It hadn't been his imagination; that tanuki he'd seen in the forest wasn't some forest animal, but a yokai in disguise. And the rumors he'd heard about the family's special connection to the forest all made sense.

"Are they here now?" Hotaru asked, peering around in the bushes. "That's who's been making those offensive sounds, is it not?"

She backed away from him. "I don't know what you're talking about."

He laughed. "You can try to pretend, but I know it's you. That's how you've been chasing away the others as well, isn't it?"

She tried to run without answering, but he grabbed onto her arm to keep her from getting away.

"Let's cut to the chase. I need a wife, and you want your free-dom. Marry me and you can live your life as you like."

She shook off his grip. "As romantic as that is, I'll pass."

She turned to walk away, but as she did she found her brother standing on the steps, staring at them both.

"What's going on here?"

"Nothing." Yuki jutted her chin and tried to walk past her brother. But as she started to walk away, her brother surprised them both by saying, "I've decided you will marry Lord Kaedemori whether you like it or not."

9

"I would rather die than marry him." Yuki pointed at the stuck-up lord in a dramatic fashion.

"I tried to give you the choice. But the time is running out. Lord Fujikawa is mobilizing. The war has begun."

"What?" Hotaru looked to Lord Fujimori.

"It seems that he's made an alliance with two other clans." The men talked of the war, and other things that should be of no concern. This was her life they were talking about; her freedom was being sold for a war her family had nothing to do with.

"This isn't our war, Riku!" Yuki shouted.

"It's our war now. Did you think chasing away the other suitors wouldn't have consequences?" He gave her a stern look and Yuki shrank away from him.

"You promised!" She growled, like a feral animal. In fact she felt something bubbling up inside her, wanting to explode.

"My duty is to the clan, Yuki." He turned his back to her to address Lord Kaedemori. "I've thought about what you've said. We cannot put our family at risk any longer. If you'll protect us against Lord Fujikawa, we can proceed—"

"I won't do it. I refuse!" Yuki snarled, cutting off her brother.

The both of them looked at her as she stood in the middle of the courtyard, hands balled into fists, her foot stomping the ground. Lord Kaedemori didn't seem bothered by her outburst. He turned to Riku and bowed. "We will speak more on this later. I must speak with my second-in-command."

Her brother nodded his head. "I understand."

Lord Kaedemori jogged away, leaving the siblings to finish their argument in private.

Riku turned to her scornfully, his normally kind face twisted in anger. She hardly recognized him. "Are you proud of yourself?"

"What happened to letting me marry for love?" she snarled.

"The circumstances have changed."

She shook her head, as if denying it would change anything. "You can't let them take me away from here. It will kill me."

"Don't be dramatic. I'm sure you'll be happy with Lord Kaedemori if you give him half a chance."

She took a step back.

Her brother reached for her. "Yuki, don't do this."

"We can fight on our own. We may be small in number but we know this forest. We can defend ourselves!"

"You know nothing of war. If you refuse, you will doom our clan."

Yuki's stomach was rolling, preparing to heave her dinner onto the floor. Anything other than marrying that monster.

"You'd blame this on me too? Just like you did with Mama. You always blamed me for her death."

Riku took another step toward her. "Yuki, you know that's not true."

She grabbed the necklace from around her neck and threw it onto the ground. "You want her? You can have her."

He stared at the necklace in the dirt. Yuki was heaving for breath, gasping, every sense of her body was alive with sensation. She could feel the tree in the center of the courtyard buzzing, ready to burst to life. It was always like this when she lost her temper. She could sense everything, from deer stripping the bark off branches in the forest, to the worm crawling under the dirt. Her head was a hornet's nest of angry buzzing. She wanted to cover her ears and shout to make it stop.

Riku knelt down and picked up the necklace off the ground. But he wasn't strong enough to stand up again. Instead he knelt on the ground in front of her.

"Mama would have wanted me to make sure you're taken care of. Who will be there for you when I'm gone?"

"Don't talk like that." Yuki's voice trembled, she couldn't bear the thought. Not now, not on top of everything else. "I can take care of myself."

"Can you? Because I am starting to question your ability to make rational decisions."

Anger boiled out of her. Buds burst all along the branches and white petals exploded, raining down upon Riku. He tilted his head back, watching them as they fell. And when his gaze rested on her, she saw his fear. Most of the time he tried to hide it, but he was just like the rest of them. He feared what she could do.

"You want me gone, then fine."

She turned and ran, scaling the wall using the vines as footholds.

Riku shouted after her but she ignored his calls. She dropped onto the ground on the other side of the wall and raced off into the forest.

Here she was free. There was no one whispering about her, commenting on her strange behavior. Here she was good enough, here she belonged. The wind moved through her hair and the chaotic buzzing turned to a slow steady heartbeat. The trees sighed as they prepared to wake from their winter slumber. Every part of her sang with the song of the forest. Riku could never understand, none of them did. It wasn't about the marriage. It was the idea of being ripped from where she belonged that made her feel like there was a hole gnawing at her gut, threatening to consume her. She was a part of the forest, and nothing could get between that.

It didn't take long for the tanuki to catch up. They leaped from tree to tree behind her. Her lungs were burning with exertion, and still she kept on going, until she reached the place where she always went when she was mad or upset. The secret place her father had shown her.

The old tree was in the center of the forest. Its large branches burst through the canopy, stretching out above all others. At a very young age, she had learned how to climb this tree. She'd never fallen, and her father used to tease that she was part monkey. But tonight, blinded by anger, she was hardly up to the second highest branch when she slipped and almost fell to the ground.

She paused for a moment to calm her breathing. Her fingers were not gripping like they normally did, but perhaps that was just the cold air making them numb. She slowed her climb, taking extra care to get to her favorite perch. It was the one which over-looked the forest.

She'd shed almost everything she was wearing back at the palace, everything but the comb the lord had given her. She should throw it away. She'd only worn it to throw it at his feet. But he'd found her out, discovered a part of her that no one had known before. How? Could he see the tanuki as she could? Even so, she didn't want to marry him.

Yuki turned the comb over in her hand and brushed a finger against the gems along the spine. The tanuki settled onto the branches around her, but sensing her mood they did not try to coax her into playing as they normally would. Suimin took his usual spot on her lap.

"What am I going to do?" She asked them as she stroked Suimin's head. Shai had curled up next to her side, and Happi lay over her feet. It was cozy with the tanuki curled around her and she could sleep outside if she wanted to.

The stars twinkled overhead. This was her home, and some over-inflated lord was not going to take her away from here. If only she could make her brother see that. Yuki put her comb back in her hair. She didn't want to lose it before she got the chance to throw it back at him and refuse his marriage offer. As she put the comb in without a mirror, she scraped it along her scalp.

The scrape stung and throbbed. It seemed to last longer than a small nick should, and as she tried to lift her hand to inspect the wound, her arm felt very weak. Her vision swam.

She squinted but couldn't focus on anything. "What is this..." But before she could finish her sentence, she was tipping over sideways and falling out of the tree.

10

Hotaru stood outside Lord Fujimori's chambers and knocked. The door opened and he was surprised to find not a servant but the Lady Fujimori. She looked equally surprised to see him.

"Oh, Lord Kaedemori, you've come rather early." She stepped out discreetly, closing the door behind her.

Once more he was entranced by the simple elegance of her every move. Those deep, bottomless eyes captured him, holding him in her spell for a moment. If it weren't for his second's cleared throat he would have remained staring at her forever.

Hotaru turned to his second-in-command. "Go and ready the men to leave."

His second bowed before hurrying to do his bidding.

"You're not leaving already, are you?" Lady Fujimori batted her lashes at him.

It was a pity she was another man's widow. But if Lord Fujimori kept to his word, then his marriage to Yuki was all but secured. Perhaps once the marriage was official he could consider other dalliances.

"There is some urgent business I must attend to back home. I only wished to speak with Lord Fujimori before I go," he said with an easy smile.

Her face crumpled before she could hide the pain in her face. She turned away, hiding her expression beneath her sleeve. But not before he could see the tears rolling down her cheek.

"Is anything the matter?" *She can't be that sad to see me go. Did Lord Fujimori die in his sleep? Where will that leave our negotiations?*

She shook her head before looking up at him with tear-filled eyes. "He fought with his sister last night, and it incited a coughing fit. He's resting now..."

Hotaru did not even realize he had taken a hold of her shoulders. There was hardly any space left between the two of them now. "I'm sorry to hear that. Is there anything I can do?"

She moved in closer, her hand tangling in the fabric of his haori. "I would not want to impose."

His vision was filled with her—her ruby lips, her pale skin. It was as if everything else fell away when he was looking at her.

"It would be no imposition at all—" He found himself leaning into her.

A violent cough tore them apart. Hotaru leaped backward as the lady stepped back, bowing her head. Lord Fujimori was looking more pale and drawn than before. The lady had not exaggerated. Judging from the dark circles under his eyes, he had not slept at all the night before. His eyes were fever-bright as he glared at Hotaru.

"What are you doing here?"

The accusations in his tone were clear. What had he been thinking getting that close to Lady Fujimori? There was something about Lady Fujimori. He seemed to lose all common sense around her.

Hotaru bowed, trying to recover from his mistake. "I came to speak with you."

Lord Fujimori was still in his night clothes, and leaning heavily onto the door frame. His fevered gaze skimmed over toward Lady

Fujimori and locked on her. She would not meet his gaze, but Hotaru recognized the look in his eyes. It was longing, and possession. Was there something more between them? He didn't want to even consider it.

His gaze returned to Hotaru. "Come in," he said in a rasping voice. Lady Fujimori motioned to follow, but he snapped, "Not you, we'll talk later."

She bowed her head, giving Hotaru one quick smile before making her way down the hall. *What have I gotten myself into with this family?* The witch insisted this was the key to winning the war. He hoped she was right.

Lord Fujimori sat down at a desk and motioned for Hotaru to join him and said, "I suppose you've come to talk about our alliance."

"I hope you haven't changed your mind from last night?"

"I must admit I'm beginning to have second thoughts. I will not give my sister to someone who does not cherish her." The anger was unwarranted, his flirtation with Lady Fujimori was nothing but that.

"You can rest assured, I would never harm your sister, or betray her in any way."

Lord Fujimori deflated a bit, the anger seeping out of him and leaving him as the shell of a man Hotaru had come to know. He rested his hands on his lap as he stared at a blank piece of parchment in front of him.

"Before we make any agreements you must know, my sister is... *different* than most people. Some call her wild."

Hotaru bit his tongue to not say something that would get him in trouble. Wild was an understatement.

"Our mother died just after she was born and well..." His hand touched a necklace on the table. It was the same he'd noticed Yuki wearing the night before. Odd. "I have never been the son my father needed. But Yuki was always happy to hunt, fish, and practice the sword. I always preferred more scholarly pursuits."

Just like Hotaru's brother Hikaru.

"I see," Hotaru replied.

"You were correct when you said our clan is in danger. Lord Fujikawa knows you are here, and he has put his army between here and your territory. The decision I make now will impact both our fates."

"Then you will let me marry Yuki?"

Lord Fujimori shook his head before falling into another coughing fit.

"I am going to give her the choice. If she chooses you then we will align ourselves with the Kaedemoris. If not, then it shall be the Fujikawas."

Hotaru clenched the edge of the table. Then his entire destiny was down to the choice of that headstrong woman?

"And she has agreed to this?"

Lord Fujimori shook his head. "She ran away after we fought last night and I haven't seen her since."

"If you would allow me, I'd like to tell her myself. I do not want her to feel like she's backed into a corner." *Because like any cornered animal she'll only bite me if I do.*

"I think that is a wise idea. But you will have to wait. She can hold onto a grudge, and it may be days before she emerges from the forest."

He didn't have days to wait. With Fujikawa throwing his weight around, the time to strike was now. "I will go and find her then."

Lord Fujimori laughed. "You can certainly try."

Hotaru was an excellent tracker, and an expert hunter. How hard could it be to find one woman? But this forest wasn't like the ones he was used to. The shadows moved in odd ways. And there was a pervasive feeling of being watched. As he crept along, he heard rustling in the treetops. He spun around, hoping to catch the watcher but there was nothing there.

He continued on, but the feeling persisted. On a hunch, he shot an arrow into a nearby tree. Something dropped from the treetops, falling onto the ground in front of him. He drew his blade and crept closer. As he did, a small tanuki turned and looked at him. Its black eyes were uncannily intelligent.

"You scared me, little man." He chuckled as he sheathed his weapon.

"If I wanted to scare you I would have transformed into a mirror," the tanuki replied.

Hotaru stumbled backward in surprise, reaching for his weapon. But something pressed a blade against his back.

"Don't even think about it." He turned slowly, and came face to face with rows of sharp teeth.

With a quick maneuver he jumped away from the yokai and drew his weapon. But as if appearing from thin air, two more of the creatures surrounded him. All of them pointed their swords at Hotaru. He was outnumbered, and outsized.

"Come quietly and you won't get hurt," they grumbled.

Hotaru nodded his head as the creatures prodded him to follow through the forest. If he fell behind at all, the poked him in the back. They brought him to a place that at first glance looked to be a massive tree but the tree had a door in it, about a quarter of Hotaru's height.

"Go in there," the creature growled.

"In there? I'd have to crawl." Hotaru scoffed. How could these huge fanged beasts get in there?

"Then crawl." The creature prodded him again.

Not wanting to challenge the yokai, Hotaru climbed onto his knees and crawled through the door. The interior was tall enough for him to hunch over. Inside was a dwelling scaled down to half his size. Seven futons lay in a row against the far wall and on top of them was an unconscious Yuki. His comb was still pulling back her ebony hair. She was drenched in sweat and her breathing was heavy.

"What's wrong with her?" Hotaru crawled over to her, lifting her head to rest on his lap.

"We do not know." A tanuki said, coming around the other side of her. Seven little tanukis wearing straw hats and a rainbow of haori and hakama lined up on the other side of her.

Hotaru placed his hand against her clammy skin. "I have to get her to a healer."

It took some finagling, but they got her out of the tiny house. If only he'd brought a horse he could get her back to the palace quicker. Then it occurred to him, the giant monsters were gone. As he looked at the small tanuki gathered around his feet, realization dawned on him. These must be her mischievous accomplices.

"I need to get her back to the palace and quick. Can you transform into a horse perhaps?"

Four of the seven joined hands, and then in a puff of smoke a saddled horse appeared. He gently placed Yuki on their back before climbing on. As soon as he swung his leg over the side, the tanuki horse took off, weaving through the forest and leaping over obstacles faster than any real horse could.

They came thundering into the courtyard, and as they did, Hotaru shouted for a healer. The crowd rushed forward, pressing in to see what was going wrong.

Yuki was pulled from his arms and whisked away into the palace beyond while he stared after her. The comb fell from her head and clattered onto the ground. He walked over and picked it up. As he did, he got the faintest whiff. *I know this smell. Night creeper. Someone tried to poison her.*

He'd given her that comb, but someone else had poisoned it. Someone was trying to frame him.

11

Yuki groaned as she woke. Her head was pounding and her mouth was dry. As she sat up, she rubbed her throbbing temples. Her brother slept, head leaning against the nearby wall. Any pain or discomfort she felt was forgotten as she crawled closer toward him. There was a faint rise and fall to his chest. With his pale skin and dark circles, he looked like a corpse.

Just to assure herself, she shook him by the shoulder. Riku cracked open a bloodshot eye and moaned. He stretched his arms which cracked and popped disconcertingly.

"Yuki, you should be resting," he said, rubbing the sleep from his eyes.

"Why are you sleeping here?" She scolded him. "What if your cough gets worse?"

He smiled faintly but it was thin and strained. "I was only dozing. I wanted to be here when you woke." He shivered and Yuki grabbed the blanket off her bed to wrap around his shoulders.

"You're going to hurt your back sleeping like that."

"You're the one who almost died and yet you're tending to me."

"Don't be stubborn. Come on, let's get you to your room

before you catch your death." She tried to stand to help her brother to his feet, but as she did her legs trembled beneath her like a newborn deer and buckled under her weight.

"Yuki, stop! You shouldn't be up and about yet." Her brother knelt in front of her, hands on her shoulders searching her for injury.

She rubbed her pounding temples once more. "Why am I so weak?" Her memory was foggy and the last thing she remembered was falling asleep in her tree.

"Please just lay down." He nudged her toward the futon. But she wasn't the type to be led anywhere.

"What happened?" She met her brother's gaze.

Her brother sighed heavily. "You were poisoned."

"Poisoned!" She knew members of the clan thought her strange. Usually they just kept their distance, but had their feelings changed and now they saw her as a threat? Yuki grasped her throat just thinking about it. She needed to be in the forest. Riku shouldn't have brought her back.

"Before you start to worry, we don't know anything yet. But I'm putting a full investigation into the matter."

Yuki drew her knees up to her chest. Who could have wanted her dead? What had she ever done to hurt someone so badly? Only one person came to mind. She'd told that stuck-up lord she'd rather die than marry him. Well apparently, he'd taken her words to heart.

Yuki felt a cold chill run down her spine. "It had to be Lord Kaedemori!"

Her brother shook his head. "It couldn't have been him. He saved your life. He found you in the forest and told the healers what poison was used. If he hadn't you would have died."

She blinked at her brother. "He did?" She couldn't believe it. But who would poison someone only to save their life? And how had he found her in the forest? No one could find her when she ran away, though many tried.

"I think you should apologize to him."

"For what?"

"You've humiliated him on more than one occasion, and yet he still rushed to rescue you. I think the least you could do is thank him for that."

"You figured it out, huh?"

"I've known you've been playing tricks to chase away all the suitors. But I think he's different, Yuki. Maybe you should give him a chance."

She drew her knees up to her chest. She hated to worry her brother, and it stung her pride to admit when she was wrong even more.

"Can't you just pass the message along to him for me?"

Riku shook his head. "I think it will be better coming from you."

Yuki exhaled heavily. There was no arguing with her brother in this case it seemed. "Fine."

He reached across and took her hand in his. "I'm sorry we fought before. I never wanted you to feel like you were unwanted. I just—" he paused as wracking coughs rippled through his body.

He didn't need to say it, she knew. He had all the same signs her father did before the end. She'd seen the blood speckled hand-kerchiefs he didn't want anyone to see. Her brother was dying. And he didn't want her to be alone once he was gone. The clan tolerated her because of who her family was. But once Riku died, there would only be the forest left for her.

She leaned across and clung to him for a moment, letting her dark thoughts go. She wouldn't upset him again.

"I'll apologize to that stuck-up lord if it will please you."

He was smiling when they broke apart. "Thank you, Yuki."

She put off meeting with the arrogant lordling for a little while longer by pretending to convalesce. But really, she was feeling much better. She'd always been quick to recover. Night creeper was a deadly poison, and most people died from it. Or at least had permanent damage from it. But she wasn't like most people. The healer was shocked, and likely afraid. Most of the clan didn't know the full extent of her power. And she wanted to keep it that way. They'd only fear her instead of thinking she was an oddity.

When she could pretend to be ill no longer she went in search of Lord Kaedemori. She found him in the main guest house, in one of the gardens, sparring with his men. She stopped to admire his form. He was a skilled fighter and without a shirt she could see the cords of muscles rippling in his back. From behind he was handsome, the problem was when he opened his mouth.

As she watched with appreciation, his bout with the soldier finished and he turned to see her staring. Yuki blushed at being caught and turned away. She decided now was not the right time to thank him for saving her life after all. She started walking the opposite way but he called out to her.

"Yuki!"

She kept on walking, hoping she could get away. Her face was on fire. *Why did I stop and stare?*

"Yuki!" he shouted again.

She spun around to face him. "You shouldn't address me so informally."

He stopped a few feet from her and his naked chest was glistening with sweat. There was a devious smirk on his face.

"Come for a rematch? I've been practicing that flip you used on me: it's very handy."

She had to force her gaze upward but focusing on his face was no better. He was too handsome and that smile was disarming.

"Ijustwantedtosaythankyouforsavingmylife." She said it all in one breath and then turned to walk away. She couldn't stand the gloating look on his face.

"I'm sorry, I didn't catch that."

She balled her hands into fists and spun around to face him once more. "Thank you." She enunciated each syllable.

"What for?" He tilted his head to the side in mock confusion.

"You know what for," she said past clenched teeth. *I will not punch him. I will not punch him.*

"Oh, for saving your life?"

She gave a stiff nod. "Now that I've said what I've come to say, I'm going."

She managed to get a few feet away before he was jogging in front of her, filling up her view with his handsome smile and well-shaped body.

"That's all I get?"

"What do you want from me? Do you think just because you saved me, I'll marry you?"

She narrowed her eyes as she glared at him. Perhaps this was all part of some convoluted plan to woo her.

He put his hands up into the air as a sign of surrender. "I know when I'm beaten. I'll be leaving here as soon as we can. My people need me, and there's no point in wasting time here if you're not interested."

She crossed her arms over her chest. Somehow, she didn't think he was telling the truth.

"But before I go, perhaps you could show me around? I've heard no one knows this forest better than you."

She narrowed her eyes further as she looked him up and down.

"Why waste your time?"

"Your brother and I have come to another agreement. I will give protection for strategic use of his forest. I thought you could help me get a lay of the land."

Yuki studied him for a moment. His expression was casual, unbothered. It had to be a trick.

"I'd rather not."

She turned to walk away.

"It's the least you could do since I saved your life."

Yuki balled her hand into a fist at her side and took a deep breath. Riku had asked her to give him a chance.

"Fine. I'll show you around, but don't try anything funny."

She stomped away, but not before he made one last comment.

"I look forward to it." There was an unnerving flirtatious note to his voice.

She ran the rest of the way back to her room and slammed the door shut for good measure before leaning against the wall, her heart hammering in her chest. Not just from the run, but the unnerving way his smile had an effect on her.

12

S unlight had not even begun to peak over the tops of the palace walls when Hotaru arrived. He'd woken well before the sunrise, too excited to sleep. There was something about Yuki that fascinated him. There had never been a woman who'd been able to resist him before. And why would someone want to kill her? He'd done some probing of his own while she was recovering from the poison. No one was openly hostile to her, though they clearly thought her obsession with the forest strange.

He hoped today would be a step in the right direction, and he wanted to use this opportunity to make his appeal to her. Yuki approached from around the corner, two horses trailing behind her. Instead of walking on leads, they followed behind her like obedient pets. She wore a plain brown hakama and haori, her hair in a braid down her back. At first glance he'd found her unassuming perhaps a bit unrefined, but there was a hidden beauty to her.

He walked toward her with a smile. "You have a way with animals it seems," he said as he nodded toward one of the horses who'd rested its head on her shoulder. Its lips gently nibbled at her ear. She patted him and gave him a treat, then the second horse almost knocked her over in his haste to get his treat as well.

Hotaru lunged forward to catch her, grabbing her by the elbow. They both froze at his touch, each of them staring at the contact before Yuki yanked her arm away, turning her back on him as she patted the horse's neck.

"Does it frighten you?" she asked softly.

"Not at all, I envy you. If only I could get my own horse to obey half as well."

She tried to hide her smile by looking away but he came around to her side, catching a glimpse of it.

"We should go." She cleared her throat.

They mounted their steeds and she led the way into the forest. Mist was kicked up by the churning of their horses' hooves as they zoomed through the forest. The place was an ominous, twisted maze of dead trees and shadows. And he was glad to have her as his guide, or else he would have gotten lost.

His horse followed hers, but he felt it shuddering beneath him. The animal was bred for the battlefield and had never been skittish. To have her shying away from every shadow made him nervous.

Meanwhile, Yuki flew through the brush. Strands of hair had been teased loose from her braid and her hair flew behind her like an ebony banner. The trees thinned, and they found a sunlight-dappled meadow. The first touches of spring were evident in the fresh grass poking from the soil. There was a creek at the far side of the meadow, with a large bent over tree. They'd been riding for a while, and this was the perfect place.

Yuki stopped in the center and leaned back in the seat of her saddle. Her head was turned upward and her hands were outstretched. Her face was flushed from the sun's kiss. There was a different energy to her in the forest. She seemed to glow, her skin was bright and her hair shinier. She was a forest goddess come to bless the mortal realm with her beauty and radiance.

She caught him staring once again, and lowered her arms to her side.

He had pulled a sack from his saddle bag. When she saw it, she frowned.

"What are you up to?"

"It's a nice day, can't we enjoy a meal together?" he said as he plopped down on the ground and patted the grass beside him.

She looked around the woods and then back at him. "You said you need to survey the land for tactical reasons."

"And I will after lunch. I'm starving."

She sat down cautiously, as far away as she could while still being within reach of the food. Hotaru set out everything and they ate in silence. She kept her gaze away from him, instead staring at the scenery. The wind rolled through the trees. Birds called to one another. Hotaru watched her. The way her eyes sparkled, or how a grain of rice clung to her chin. A part of him wanted to reach over and remove it for her, but he feared that wouldn't be welcome.

It almost seemed cruel to take her from this place. And for the first time, he really thought about what it would mean to make her his wife and have her bear his children. He hadn't even realized he was staring at her until she looked up to meet his gaze. She smiled faintly, perhaps embarrassed about being stared at.

She flopped back onto the ground. "It's a beautiful day," she said with a sigh.

"I was a bit afraid of this place when I first arrived to be honest, but I've seen the beauty of it." He stared at her profile, she was intent on the clouds rolling overhead.

She turned to look at him, and realizing he'd been caught staring at her again, he got up to check on the horses. Not that they needed any checking on. They were content to nibble on the sweet grass.

"Are you still?" she asked.

He leaned against the horse as he faced her. "No, not anymore."

She nodded her head. He wasn't sure if that was a good thing or a bad thing. It was difficult to tell with her.

They got on their horses again and this time she took him on a more meandering trip through the forest. They talked and laughed together while she pointed out the various flora and fauna.

They headed up a gentle slope and at the top was a massive tree. The branches reached over the tops of the smaller trees, dwarfing them in size. Unlike much of the forest around it, fresh green leaves had begun to fill in its branches and lend shade. While Hotaru tied the horses to a nearby low hanging branch, Yuki disappeared. Hotaru turned around to look for her.

Then her head popped in front of him, hanging upside down with her braid swinging. She shouted, causing him to stumble backward before they both laughed.

"Join me, unless you're afraid of heights." She disappeared into the trees, and Hotaru scrambled to climb the giant tree after her. She was standing on one of the higher branches, leaning against the trunk.

He joined her on the branch where they could see the forest roll along the horizon. When he first arrived the forest had seemed dark and ominous, but from this vantage point it was easy to see why Yuki loved this place. Green swirled through the forest as spring awoke from its long slumber. In the distance, the tops of the palace burst from the center of the forest. The sun was low in the sky, already starting its descent and the sky was painted pink and orange in broad brush strokes.

"It's beautiful," he said

"This is my favorite place in the whole valley."

"I can see why. Thank you for showing me."

She turned to face him. "I know you've come looking for a wife. And—" she seemed to struggle with her words.

"You don't have to apologize. I understand." He should have told her about the deal, but he couldn't find the right words. He didn't want to ruin this moment. "How could you want to leave this place?" He gestured toward the scenery.

She crossed her arms over her chest. "Your pretty smooth. I almost fell for it."

He laughed. "I mean it. This place is like something out of a dream."

She looked back to the horizon. "It's not just the forest. My brother is all I have left. He needs me here."

"He has his stepmother."

"She's not our mother. She's not blood," Yuki snapped. There were tears in her eyes and he so badly wanted to wipe those tears away. They both left the rest unsaid; her brother wouldn't make it until the next winter. But he didn't have that kind of time to wait for her. Even if he could convince her to fall in love with him, neither of them had time.

She turned her back to him to wipe her tears away. And he left her with her distance until she had composed herself.

They climbed back down after that and rode back home in silence through the growing darkness.

When they returned to the palace he bowed to her and said, "Thank you, it was a lovely day."

She was somber but not rude when she said, "It was a good time. You're not as terrible as I thought."

He smiled at the almost compliment. "There's one more thing. Wait here."

He ran back to his room to get the other present he had brought for her. It seemed silly given what he knew about her now, but he couldn't imagine giving it to anyone else.

He was relieved to find her still waiting in the courtyard when he returned, and he handed her the kimono he had brought.

"I know this is probably not a gift to your liking."

She brushed her hands over the fabric. "No, I do like it. I just —" She blushed prettily. "I never had a mother who taught me how to wear these sorts of things."

"You don't have to. I won't be offended." He reached to take it back but she pulled it from his grip.

"No, I like it. That is to say, I'll wear it, before you go."

And there it was, the unspoken promise that had kept the peace between them. It was another chance to come clean, but he found his tongue caught on the words. "I would like that," he said.

They lingered a moment. There wasn't much more that could be said. And yet neither one of them would leave.

"Well, good night," she said.

"Good night." He turned to walk away and on impulse he turned around, just to see if she were watching him go. And to his surprise she was still watching him. But when he caught her, she scurried away.

He couldn't help but smile at the thought.

13

Yuki stared at the kimono laying on her futon. It was beautiful – bright yellow with large red and blue flowers splashed across it. And a dark blue obi to tie it off. She'd never really worn things like this. It had never suited her style. Delicate fabrics and bright colors had no place in the forest where they could be torn or dirtied. Despite this not being something she was used to, she wanted to wear it. In the forest today she saw a different side of Hotaru: the way he absorbed the beauty of the forest with a reverent awe. And because she felt the forest respond to him in a way she'd never seen before. It felt as if he were a part of it. It felt like he belonged.

As much as she wanted to wear it to say thank you for saving her life, it didn't feel right for her. She was better suited for muted browns and greens—colors that blended in, not stood out. She preferred to sink into the shadows. Everyone would see her in this, and they would talk. She'd learned to ignore the gossip of the clan and they mostly ignored her. In this there would be plenty of talk and she wasn't sure she could handle it.

Yuki picked up the kimono, holding it up, letting the light catch the vibrant yellow. The bright colorful flowers would be better suited to a woman who had effortless beauty. Someone like her stepmother. Not Yuki, whose hands were calloused and had jagged nails from climbing trees, and hair that was hardly in anything other than a braid.

She set it back down and squatted next to it, poking at it as if it was alive and she feared it would bite her. It remained lifeless on her bed. *What am I thinking? I can't wear this. What if he gets the wrong idea?* She turned to go through her small wardrobe, one of her everyday clothes would be fine. *He said he wouldn't be offended if I didn't wear it.* Yuki grabbed the handle to her bureau. *But I said I would wear it.* She shook her head. It wasn't like he mattered. He'd leave like all the rest and she'd never see him again. The realization left her with a squirming sensation in her gut. She shook herself. She was being silly.

"Ha! He really thought I'd wear something like this."

She looked back at the kimono longingly. It was beautiful. The kimono started to wiggle and Yuki stumbled backward to reach for a blunt object to strike it with when a small black nose poked out.

She let go a sigh of relief. "Oh, Baka, you scared me!" He wriggled out of the kimono and came over to her as six more tanuki appeared in small puffs of smoke.

"What game are we going to play tonight?" Kushami asked before turning to sneeze.

"Maybe we should paint a mustache on him?" suggested Happi.

"Or set him on fire again!" Okatsu cheered.

"That is a great idea!" yawned Suimin.

They all danced around her, shouting out ideas for how to torture Hotaru, their stripped tails wagging. Only Kashikoi sat at the edge of the group looking pensive.

"I don't think we should," he said.

His brothers all spun toward him, heads tilted inquisitively. "But he's trying to take away our Yuki. We should make sure he leaves for good," said Shai.

"Have you forgotten? He saved Yuki!" Kashikoi countered.

The tanuki muttered to one another as Yuki knelt down among them. She ruffled the top of Kashikoi's head. "He's right. Hotaru isn't a bad man. And besides, he's leaving soon anyway."

There were small groans of complaint from the tanuki, but she let them play around her room as she decided what to wear.

"This is pretty," said Shai.

"I want to see," said Happi, followed by agreements from several of his brothers. They all took a corner and started tugging on the kimono.

"Don't, you'll rip it." She snatched it out of their tiny paws.

"You never cared about pretty things before," said Kashikoi. He was always the most clever of them. She smoothed out the wrinkles in the fabric the tanuki had made.

"It was a gift," she said before setting it on top of the chest out of the reach of the tanuki.

"Perhaps you should wear it," he said.

She pulled a face. "I wouldn't even know how to put it on."

"Ask your stepmother, she's always wearing pretty things," Happi suggested.

Yuki stared at the kimono. The tanuki couldn't understand the complicated relationship she and her stepmother shared. She and her stepmother hardly spoke, except when it was strictly necessary. And even then, Yuki was often bordering on rude. She really wanted to wear the kimono and didn't know where else to turn. *He saved my life, the least I can do is wear the present he gave me.*

Swallowing her pride, she hurried out of the room and down the hall to her stepmother's chamber. They'd never been close. Her father always said he never wanted to remarry. His heart had room for only one woman and that was her mother. Then a year ago he had taken another wife and it was as if her mother never existed. It felt like a betrayal. That was when she knew love was just an illusion.

The door felt like an impenetrable barrier. How could she ask a woman she barely liked for help? Yuki was about to walk away when the door slid open.

"Yuki?" her stepmother said.

Yuki spun around and held up the wrinkled bundle of fabric in her arms.

"Help."

Her stepmother laughed. "Oh, what a pretty kimono. Where did you get it from?"

She didn't want to admit it was from Hotaru. Her stepmother would surely make the wrong connections and if it got back to her brother, he might get the wrong impression and think she was considering him as a husband.

But she couldn't think of a good lie and instead said, "From a friend."

Her stepmother gave her a knowing smile. "This color would be beautiful on you. Let me help you put it on."

She gestured for Yuki to come in. Yuki stood in the center of the room, looking around. She'd never been in her room before. It was decorated in a way that wasn't surprising; she had a painted screen in one corner and a large, rare mirror against the far wall.

While her stepmother put on the layers of clothes to the kimono, Yuki watched herself in the mirror. She'd never really looked at herself before, other than the odd reflection in a pool of water. But as the kimono went on, and then her stepmother dressed and styled her hair, she saw a stranger look back at her. She turned her head from side to side.

"Is it really me?" she asked.

Her stepmother put her hands on her shoulders. "Yes, it's you."

Both their faces stared back at them from the mirror. Yuki couldn't help but compare herself to her stepmother, who was pale and beautiful, while Yuki's skin was tanned and unrefined.

"I'm glad you came to me for help." Her stepmother squeezed her shoulders.

Yuki turned away from the mirror, unable to stare at her

subpar reflection any longer. Perhaps it had been a mistake to wear this.

"Thank you." Yuki headed for the door.

"Your father would have been proud of you."

Yuki froze in the doorway, unable to acknowledge her step-mother other than giving a quick nod and then she was out in the hall.

The kimono made walking difficult and she was forced to take small, delicate steps. It should have looked graceful but she felt more like a baby animal learning to walk for the first time. As soon as they entered the dining hall, she found herself searching out Hotaru. He sat at the head of the room, talking with her brother. When she entered his head turned and his mouth dropped open.

A blush crept across her cheeks. As she took her slow wobbling steps to her seat beside her brother, he kept his eyes on her. She wanted to snap at him for staring but the weight of his gaze and the heavy obi on her diaphragm made it almost impossible. She had to concentrate on breathing.

Yuki took her seat and her brother leaned in close to her. "You look beautiful, Yuki. I almost didn't recognize you."

She gave her brother a gentle slap. He smiled before turning to speak with her stepmother.

She peeked at Hotaru from the corner of her eye, and he was still watching her, mouth agape.

"You're going to catch flies if you keep your mouth open like that," she teased.

He clamped his mouth shut.

No man had ever looked at her that way before. Was this why women dressed this way? But none of the clansmen were looking at her. There had been some good-natured teasing when she entered the room, but Hotaru couldn't take his eyes off her. And the idea made her chest tight. Almost as if she couldn't breathe. She turned away, too embarrassed. Just for tonight, she'd like to pretend to be someone else. The kind of girl who was admired by men, who was beautiful without trying. And who could believe in love.

Across the room musicians played softly, and though Hotaru said nothing, she kept catching him watching her.

As she ate she found she had less appetite than she thought. All the layers of fabric were pressing down on her. Her face was clammy and she was struggling to keep her eyes open. Suddenly everything around her swayed.

I must be too hot in this. The magic of the kimono was wearing thin. She needed to get back in her own clothes. She got up to make her way to the door, but as she walked the constricting feeling only got worse.

She lost balance again and had to lean on the wall. She hadn't even heard Hotaru come up behind her, but felt his hand on the small of her back.

"What's wrong?" he asked.

She shook her head and kept going but the edges of her vision were going dark. She stumbled and fell. She couldn't breathe. She tried to take a deep breath but couldn't. It felt as if something was pressing down on her chest. *It's the kimono, it's too tight.* She clawed at the obi, but couldn't pull it loose.

She slid down the wall, collapsing onto her knees. Each attempt to breathe wasn't enough, it felt like hundreds of daggers piercing her insides. Hotaru grabbed her shoulders, his face filled her vision.

"Yuki, what is it?"

She couldn't make a sound. Even her movements were sluggish as her body was deprived of air. Her vision was going black as she slumped over into Hotaru's arms.

14

"Yuki!" Hotaru shook her and her head lolled back and forth. She wasn't breathing.

The clansmen gathered around him. They were all whispering, making accusations.

Hotaru, in a panic, scanned her body, wondering what had caused this. She'd been clawing at her kimono. He removed a knife that he kept hidden and laid Yuki on the ground.

"What are you doing? We need to get a healer." Lord Fujimori had pressed to the front of the crowd.

Hotaru shook his head. "There's no time for that."

His knife caught under the edge of her obi and sliced through the delicate silk. It was harder to tear apart than it should have been. It was his first indication something was very wrong. Hotaru pulled back the layers, slicing them one at a time until she was in nothing but her underlayer.

She gasped for breath and coughed violently. Lord Fujimori collapsed at her side, pulling her into his embrace.

"Yuki, are you alright?" She clung onto her brother, taking a few moments to catch her breath. When she saw Hotaru she pointed her finger in his direction.

"You did this to me?"

All eyes turned as one on Hotaru, and he felt their collective stares upon him.

"I just saved your life, again!"

The healer arrived just then and before they could continue their conversation, Yuki was whisked away to be examined. The party was broken up, but Lord Fujimori wasn't done with Hotaru. He placed his hand on his shoulder. "We need to speak, alone."

Hotaru bowed his head in understanding. He was escorted by a few of the clansmen. His own men rose up to defend him but Hotaru raised a hand to still them. This was all a misunderstanding, surely.

He was brought to Lord Fujimori's chamber and left there to wait. Sitting alone in the dimly lit room, he felt a bit like a prisoner. He had to find out who was trying to frame him. Could there be a Fujikawa spy somewhere in the palace?

The door slid open and soft footsteps crossed the room. But Hotaru kept his gaze forward, he would maintain some dignity.

"Thank you for meeting with me," Lord Fujimori said as he sat down. He leaned over and coughed, his entire body shaking.

Hotaru watched him, wondering if there were something else he could be doing other than just sitting here. It seemed in just the short time he'd been there, Lord Fujimori had gotten worse. Even now he looked as if he were being propped up like a puppet. But who was pulling the strings? That's what he wanted to know.

"Yuki has said the kimono was cursed. She did not realize it was trying to suffocate her until it was too late. And that you gave it to her."

Hotaru clenched his teeth together. "It troubles me that the gifts I brought were used in this way."

The lord met his gaze. Despite the illness that was withering his body, he had steel there.

"That is what I wanted to speak with you about."

Hotaru's hand clenched into a fist at his side. Just as he had feared, they thought he had been the one who tried to kill Yuki.

"Are you asking if I tried to kill your sister?" Hotaru could hardly keep the snarl out of his voice. "I came here with the intention of making an alliance." He tried to keep his voice calm but found it rising nonetheless.

The lord just stared at him for a moment. "I am making no accusations, but I cannot let you leave until this matter is settled. The entire palace will be questioned."

But he was the prime suspect of course. This had to be a plot from Lord Fujikawa, trying to ruin his negotiations. When he embarked on this war, he had always envisioned bringing glory and honor to his clan. Now everything was falling apart.

"If you've nothing else to say." Hotaru stood up.

"I mean no offense, but she is all I have. I've got to protect her."

"Then maybe you should start looking for the killer, instead of targeting the wrong man." He let his tongue get away from him.

As Lord Fujimori stared at him, Hotaru knew he'd already made up his mind. He would have thought the same if it were to happen in his household. The most obvious suspect was usually the right one.

Hotaru stormed out of the room, brushing past servants who shrunk away from him, as if he were a monster. He'd already questioned his own men after the comb had been poisoned and he had no reason to doubt them. The gifts were locked in his room. No one had gone near them since they'd arrived.

While he was scowling and considering his problem, he spotted Yuki down the hall. The healer had released her already. She'd changed into her plain brown haori and hakama and was walking in his direction. But when she spotted him, she froze like a frightened animal. He waved to her. She returned it with a cold and unfeeling stare. It hit him like a knife to the gut.

After their ride through the forest, he thought they'd grown closer. A foolish part of him had hoped she would trust him enough to let him explain his side. But just like her brother, she'd already made up her mind.

She turned and walked the opposite way. He didn't try and chase after her this time. He stalked back to his chamber. He threw open the door and slammed it shut again. And stared at it for a moment. There was so much riding on this alliance. His reputation, namely. But how could he prove his innocence?

There was a cold chill on the back of his neck. He wasn't alone. He should have known. He turned to see the witch waiting for him, that infernal smile on her face. The witch always appeared when it suited her. She'd come to him when he'd taken control over the clan. Her assistance had been invaluable—at first. She knew things about his enemies, and about the yokai.

He was too weary for her riddles today.

"We'll need to find another girl; the alliance isn't going to happen," he said.

"There is no other girl. There is no other way."

"If you want her so badly why don't you try and get her to marry you? Because she thinks I'm trying to kill her."

"Proud Hotaru, you wanted more than anything to be an elder. And now that you are, you give up so easily. Will you let one obstacle stop you from achieving all you hoped for?"

"I don't see what's so special about these people. And a tiny territory in the middle of the forest."

"This place, these people, are blessed by the divine. No one more so than the girl. That is why it is imperative we get her. Her gifts could win your war."

Hotaru scoffed. He'd seen what the witch could do. Yuki was a little strange, but she did not have any power like the witch. "I think you have the wrong girl. She's just a wild woman."

The old woman shook her head, and the bells on her staff jingled.

"There is more to this family than meets the eye. That is why someone is trying to force you apart."

"Do you know who it is?"

The old woman shook her head. "Their identity is hidden from me, but I can guarantee we are not the only ones looking for power here."

"Why can't you just sing a song and summon me an army?"

She chuckled. "Even my power is not limitless, and it has been many centuries since I last replenished it. I am growing weaker in my old age."

"Even so, I don't think she'll trust me again."

"Isn't that what you're good at, making women fall in love with you?"

"She's not like other women." Hotaru ran his hands through his hair in exasperation. "You're a woman, what would you suggest?"

She smiled in a way that made his teeth chatter. "Maybe you should try getting to know her better."

"Thanks, real helpful."

"Don't waste time. Lord Fujikawa's army draws ever closer."

He turned once more to the witch but she was gone. Hotaru stared at the place where she had been. She was as useless as usual. He was going to have to resolve this himself by finding out who was trying to frame him.

15

By her brother's orders, Yuki was forbidden from going into the forest. Being trapped within the palace walls only made her more restless. She tried to stay in her room to avoid running into Hotaru, but in the end she was pacing the length of her room, tripping over tanuki who were trying to get her to play.

In the end, she went to the garden. Sitting beside the pond was a sad shadow of the wild, untamed places outside the palace walls. But what other choice did she have? Normally she would have disobeyed her brother's orders, but his health was a concern. She couldn't help but feel like it was her fault the circles under his eyes had gotten darker and that his cough was getting worse. He couldn't rest and recover if he were worrying about her. So she succumbed to her imprisonment. But it didn't mean she'd like it.

Footsteps approached from behind her. She spun around, expecting a masked assassin holding a blade, but saw Hotaru instead.

"What are you doing here? Are you going to push me into the pond and pretend you didn't so you can save me from drowning?"

There was a pained look on his face, as if she had slapped him. But he held her gaze, not looking away. It felt very much like hunting a predator. The first one to look away would be the one to lose.

"I want to help you find out who did this."

She forced a laugh. "Very clever. I'm sure you've already picked out some innocent among your men to frame for your crimes. Are you hoping once this little charade plays out I'll leap into your arms and want to marry you?"

"This isn't about the marriage," he snapped.

"I know your type. I know what you're after. You want the power we have to wage whatever wars you will. But I'm not going to be some prize."

"You have no idea what I'm up against."

"It must be very hard to be a spoiled lord. You've gotten everything you've ever wanted your whole life. But you can't have me."

His face flushed with anger, and it gave her a thrill to see it. She had almost fallen for his games. And that's what bothered her the most. To think she felt sorry to see him go.

"Have you ever considered what it's like for your brother? What he's up against? The trouble you've caused him with these games?" His words were raw, and angry. But not at her, it was something else.

"Don't you dare speak about my brother." She marched toward him, prepared to strike him but he caught her wrist before she could.

"I'm going to find out who did this to you. Not for you but to clear my own name."

He dropped her hand and stalked away.

"Good, leave!" She shouted. But he did not once look back at her. Even after he was gone, she continued to stare at the space where he had been.

It was all an act. It had to be. She wouldn't consider the alternative.

She sat back down at the pond, more angry at herself for continuing to let him get a rise out of her than anything else. Her brother shouldn't even let him wander around the palace in this manner. He should be locked up for what he did. She watched the koi fish circle inside the pond, her own thoughts following similar pathways.

One of the koi came to the water's surface and spit water into her face.

"Ugh." She jumped up as she wiped the water from her face and shook off her wet clothes. "That's not funny, Happi," she said to the swimming tanuki.

She walked away from the pond and realized what had looked like a decorative plant before turned out to be Okatsu. A rock, a bush, and a bird sitting on the nearby wall all transformed into tanuki as she passed.

"Should we play a game with him again?" asked Okatsu, glaring in the direction he had gone, his small arms crossed over his chest.

She shook her head. "He's not worth the trouble."

"But he made you cry," Shai said. He'd crawled into her lap and brushed away a stray tear from her lashes. She rubbed the palm of her hand against her face to get rid of it. It wasn't him, but what he said. He was right, she never thought about how her resistance to marrying had put her brother in a difficult situation. All the clans of the region were at war, she knew that. And if she were to marry, it could keep the entire family safe. *If I get married, it will be anyone but him.*

"I don't care about him. All I want is to find proof of what he's done."

"We can do that," Kashikoi chirped.

She looked at the seven tanuki in front of her. They were full of mischief and caused more problems than they solved. Unleashing them on the palace might not be the wisest of ideas. But their ability to disguise themselves meant they could get into places she could not, and learn things Hotaru might be keeping hidden.

"I think we have a little game we can play. Follow the lord around, see what he's doing and report back to me."

They nodded their heads a little too eagerly, and she added on one more instruction. "And don't cause any trouble. I don't want my brother finding out."

"We will be good," they said, crossing their hands over their hearts. Yuki shooed them away. Either this was her greatest idea or her stupidest. At the very least she could cause that arrogant lord a little bit of trouble.

Yuki spent the rest of the day subconsciously waiting for the tanuki to report back to her. She hadn't heard of anything broken, or any great catastrophes, so that was a relief at least. But as the day wore on and there was still no word, she started to get more and more concerned.

She resumed pacing in her room just before dinner, and considering skipping it to go and track the rascals down, when there was a loud pop and seven tanuki plopped onto the tatami flooring in front of her.

She knelt down. "So did you find any proof?" she asked them.

Kashikoi shook his head, a small frown on his furry face. "We followed him all day. But there's no proof."

"He walks around like this a lot," Happi said, transforming into an almost perfect replica of Hotaru, except with a striped tail. The fake Hotaru walked back and forth, scowling as he placed a hand on his chin.

Yuki laughed to see the copy. She tilted her head, examining it. He wasn't as handsome with a scowl and tail she decided. But what was she thinking? He was a manipulative jerk!

"And he talks a lot," Shai piped up. "Questions, questions, Yuki this, Yuki that." He waggled his finger this way and that, also mimicking a scowl as he paced.

The other tanuki thought this quite funny and pretty soon she had seven Hotaru's with varying accuracy pacing her room. The sight was too much and Yuki fell over, clutching her side as she laughed.

Once she composed herself, and wrangled the tanuki into listening she asked, "What sort of questions?" Yuki couldn't help but be curious.

"He asks about you. Who likes you, but everyone does."

She nodded. That's what the tanuki thought. She wouldn't correct them. "But he asks about powers. About your sight," said Kushami with a yawn. All the activity had tuckered him out and he was curled up in her lap. She stroked his fur as she thought.

"He knows about my power? How?"

They shrugged. "Maybe he sees too?"

That was possible, though she'd never met someone like her. Everyone in the palace just tolerated her strangeness. They didn't question her. But they didn't really accept her either. But he had known about the yokai, and the forest accepted him. Could it be possible there was someone like her? *That doesn't change the fact that he tried to kill me.* There was only one way to prove her theory.

"I'm going to watch him too."

16

Talking to the Fujimori clansmen was much more difficult than he thought it would be. None of them were willing to speak about Yuki and it was clear from their abrupt answers and eagerness to get away from him, they were all convinced of his guilt already.

More than once he turned around, intending to explain everything to Yuki. But his pride kept getting in the way. He finally had a stroke of luck when he came across one of the kitchen maids struggling with a large pile of dishes. He rushed over to take the load from her hands.

The maid couldn't see beyond the stack, and when she was freed of her burden her eyes grew wide.

"My lord," she said, blushing at his charming smile and she bowed deeply to him.

"Let me help you with that."

"Oh no, my lord that isn't appropriate."

He leaned in close to whisper in her ear. "We don't have to tell anyone."

She turned so red he thought steam would come out of her ears.

"Where to?" he asked.

She gestured vaguely to her right, and Hotaru juggled the wobbling stack in the direction she had indicated. She hurried to catch up with him, and he tried putting her at ease by filling the silence with small talk. She led him to the kitchens where maids were running in and out and cooks were rushing back and forth, preparing for the evening meal.

One maid passed them on her way out, carrying a tea set, but the aroma of the leaves was nothing he'd ever smelled before. The maid caught him staring and blushed, pausing to bow her head to him. He gave her a smile and she almost dropped the tray she was holding.

"Hurry up and bring that to Lord Fujimori!" shouted a ruddy-faced middle-aged woman who was standing in the doorway.

The maid scurried to do as she was told while the older woman looked him up and down.

"Why is he doing your duties for you?" she asked the maid he had helped.

The girl quickly took the stack from him and rushed inside. Hotaru grinned at the woman who didn't smile back.

"What tea was that girl bringing? It smelled delightful."

The old woman narrowed her eyes at him. "It's a special brew the Lady Fujimori has us make to help his cough."

Hotaru nodded, pretending it was of interest. The old woman turned back to her work. There was a cook-fire a few feet away, with a large pot boiling over. He didn't dare enter the kitchen, fearing the contents of the pot would end up on him if he did, but he lingered in the doorway to chat with the woman.

"Have you worked here long?" he asked her.

She wouldn't face him as she said while she stirred a pot of soup. "My whole life."

"A pretty girl like you?"

The old woman scoffed. "What is it you want?

"I have some questions, if you don't mind answering."

"I do and I won't." She turned to cut up vegetables on a nearby table. Hotaru took a chance and followed her into the kitchen. She glared at him but didn't tell him to leave. He was still a visiting elder after all, it wasn't her position to tell him what to do.

"What is this illness the young lord has?"

One of the assistants brought a ladle over to her. She took a taste of some sauce, nodded her head and gave instructions to change it to her liking.

"What's it matter to you?" she said when Hotaru didn't take a hint and leave.

"Like I said, I'm curious."

The old woman turned to look at him, hands on hips, her eyes narrowed as she scanned him up and down.

"If you think I'm going to betray the family whose service I've been in for decades, then you're more a fool than you look."

"Decades? You don't look a day over thirty."

"Get out of my kitchen." The old woman picked up a very large knife. Hotaru put his hands up in the air, a sign of surrender as he slowly backed out of the kitchen. He was turning around to leave, when he found Yuki standing in the doorway.

She looked like she wanted to be mad, but was amused by the cook kicking him out of the kitchen.

She bit her lip and then cleared her throat. "What do you think you're doing?"

"I was wondering when you were going to come out of hiding." He smirked.

She flushed but didn't drop her gaze. "Why are you sneaking around the kitchen? Are you going to poison my brother next?"

He brushed past her on his way out of the kitchen, not giving Yuki the satisfaction of an answer. He didn't need to explain himself. But to his surprise, she chased after him.

"I asked you a question," she said in a huff.

He turned to look at her. "I thought you wanted nothing to do with me."

She scowled. "You've been asking around about me."

"I have."

"Why?"

"As you heard me telling your lovely cook. I'm curious. Why would anyone want to kill you? You seem nice enough. Though you do have a bit of a temper."

She crossed her arms over her chest. "No one wants to murder me."

"Clearly someone does." And there it was, the hint of doubt he had been hoping for. It was a relief to know she hadn't completely written him off.

"Alright, I'll bite. Say someone is trying to kill me. What does that have to do with the maids?"

He held up his hand and then looked around, crooking his finger to tempt her closer. She leaned in toward him. There was an earthy floral scent to her, and her lips were tantalizingly close. He needed to tread carefully if he didn't want to get slapped. But he couldn't resist the urge to tease her, if only a little.

"The maids can get anywhere in the palace. They see everything."

She pulled back. "That's it? That's your big secret."

He shrugged his shoulders. "I didn't say it was revolutionary."

"And for a moment I almost believed you hadn't planned this all from the start."

His ploy had backfired and he blurted out his thoughts. "I gave those things to you, it's true. But I swear they were untainted when they left my hands. I wouldn't stoop so low as to risk your life just to trick you into falling in love with me. I have some dignity."

She froze and for a moment he thought she was going to slap him. But she turned to face him. "Go on."

He exhaled in relief. "Who would have had access to your room?"

Yuki pondered this for a moment. "Well any of the servants or my family. But none of them would have."

He shook his head. "That is your first mistake. You have to look beyond yourself. Anyone could be the culprit here. Even those you trust more than anything."

"My brother would not have done something like this!"

Hotaru held up his hands. "And I am laying no blame here. I just want you to keep an open mind is all."

She eased back a bit but there was wariness in her eyes.

"Even if you do prove your innocence, it won't change anything."

"Noted. So what do you say? Do you think you can work with me?"

She looked at him for a moment before nodding her head. "Alright. Let's work together."

17

Yuki paced the length of her room. Why had she agreed to work with him? It was clearly part of his convoluted plan to seduce her. But as much as she tried to convince herself this was the truth, she couldn't shake the look in his eyes. He seemed sincere. If he were planning on trying to seduce her, would he really go to such lengths?

There was a knock at the door and she almost jumped out of her skin.

"Yuki, it's me," Hotaru said from the other side.

She glared at the door, wondering if it was too late to change her mind about trusting him.

"Are you going to let me in?" Hotaru said.

Yuki exhaled heavily before going to open the door. He greeted her with a grin, that damn smile. It would be her undoing. It left all her defenses at her feet and made her stomach flop uncomfortably. *Get it together, don't fall for his charm.*

"Shall we?" He gestured down the hall and she followed him out.

"Where are we going exactly?"

"We're going to follow the staff around."

She shook her head. "What good will that do?"

"The only people who have had access to the presents were my men on the transport and your servants."

"Perhaps you should question your own men."

"I have, and I've found no evidence of their involvement."

"I highly doubt the servants here would want to hurt me. They're practically family."

He shook his head. "Let's just watch and see."

She sighed heavily. But she'd agreed to work with him, the least she could do was play along. Perhaps she'd find evidence to condemn him—she hadn't completely ruled out his guilt.

His grand plan was not sophisticated. They mostly followed around the service under the guises of Yuki giving him a tour of the palace. When they were in an empty room where a servant was cleaning, she was showing him a mural. When a servant was wiping down a hallway, they were admiring the barren trees in the nearby garden. It was foolishness, all of it. All she got were strange looks from the servants who must have thought she'd gone mad. Everyone knew she had no interest in marrying, and that she'd even entertain a suitor was completely out of character.

After hours of fruitless spying, Hotaru made an announcement. "This won't work if they know we're watching."

"Clearly." Yuki rolled her eyes.

"I think we should set a trap."

Yuki narrowed her eyes at him. "You're not going to use me as bait, are you?"

He waved away her concern with a flap of his hand. "I wouldn't dream of it. The would-be assassin is trying to make me look like the culprit, so all we must do is give you another gift and wait for it to be tampered with."

"How do you intend to do that?"

"You'll see. Wait here."

Hotaru jogged off, leaving her standing in the middle of the hallway. She watched him go with a confused expression. They weren't far from his rooms, and when she saw him go into his chamber, she started to get an inkling of what he was planning. Hotaru returned a few minutes later with a present for her. It was a jade bracelet with a dragon carved into the band.

"Let me put it on you." He held it out.

After his first two presents had nearly killed her, she was hesitant to try on another. What if he had done something to this one too?

"I'd rather not," she said, looking at the bracelet dubiously.

"Want me to try it on first?"

He slipped the bracelet onto his wrist and flapped his wrist around in a dramatic fashion. "What do you think? Does it suit me?"

The flamboyant way in which he fluttered his eyelashes was her undoing and she burst out into peals of laughter. She covered her mouth, she didn't want to give him the satisfaction.

But the smile on her face and his accompanying laughter only made it worse. When they had both gotten over the giggles, he took her wrist and put the bracelet on her. His hand lingered for a moment, his thumb pressed against her pulse. She should pull away, but there was something warm and comforting about his grip.

"See, I'm not so bad." He smirked at her.

She yanked her hand away, clutching her wrist, which was still warm from his touch. "I suppose not."

They returned to her room, and said their goodbyes. When she was alone, Yuki spun the bracelet around her wrist. She hated to admit it, but Hotaru could be charming when he wanted, and so far, she felt no ill effects from his gift. Maybe he had been telling the truth. She took it off and set it down on one of her chests before leaving the room.

What if nothing happens? Then what? If they couldn't find another culprit, then it had to be Hotaru. And she didn't want to think about that. As she headed down the hall, someone grabbed her wrist. Yuki spun, ready to defend herself, but saw Hotaru crouching in the shadows, a finger pressed to his lips. He pulled her down next to where he was hiding. The bush they were sitting in gave them the perfect view of her room door. If anyone were to go in, they would see them.

"Now what?" she asked.

"We wait." He grinned at her.

And so they sat and watched her room, more than once someone walked by. But each time they tensed and prepared to apprehend them, the person walked on by.

Feeling restless, Yuki shifted from foot to foot. It wasn't just sitting still, she was dangerously close to Hotaru. The heat of his body and his masculine scent were driving her to distraction. Why did he have to smell so good?

"This is terribly boring, aren't you uncomfortable?" She looked over at Hotaru. He'd hardly moved a muscle since they'd began.

"I'm good at staying still. It's something my father made sure to beat into me at an early age." It was such a casual comment, she thought it might be a joke. But he wasn't smiling. His mouth was a firm line, his gaze forward.

"Did he hit you often?"

He shrugged. "Only when I earned it." He turned and gave her a cheeky smile. "Which he felt was often."

The glib way in which he spoke of his father's cruelty broke her heart.

"That's awful."

Hotaru shrugged. "It's in the past."

"That's no way to treat his heir..."

"I wasn't the heir. My older brother was set to rule after my father..." He hesitated. "But he gave up his place to me."

There was more to the story, she was certain, but the telling warranted a greater level of intimacy than they shared.

"Oh," she said, feeling awkward having pried.

"You don't have to pity me." His eyes met hers, she saw pain and a longing for someone to understand, to care. She looked away.

She shifted again, and wanting to fill the silence, she said, "My father never struck me, but I don't think he really knew what to do with me."

He cocked his head to one side to listen to her better, while keeping his eyes on the door. She wasn't sure why she was telling him other than to repay him for his own story.

"My mother died giving birth to me. And my father was much better at being a fighter than anything else. So he raised my brother and I the same. But everyone thought I was strange growing up. Not a lady, too wild, too in love with the forest. My family has always felt a connection to the forest, but for me even more so."

"That's what I like about you though." He said it casually without looking at her.

"I thought you promised not to talk about those sort of things." Her entire body was as tight as a bowstring, while her stomach twisted in knots.

"I promised not to talk about marriage. I never said I wouldn't admire you." He gave her another cheeky grin.

She was about to scold him when they heard footsteps on the walkway nearby. A shadowy figure was creeping toward her room. Their backs were to the person and she couldn't see if it was a man or a woman, let alone who it was. The figure looked both ways before opening the door just wide enough to slip inside.

"Well, there's our cue."

18

They burst into the room. A woman had her back to them. But as they entered she turned around to face them. It was the same maid he had run into in the hall carrying the large stack of dishes.

"Who are you?" Yuki challenged. "You're not one of the clan."

The maid dropped the jade bracelet onto the ground and rushed toward them, her mouth unhinging as she did, revealing rows and rows of razor-sharp teeth. The yokai lunged for Yuki, but Hotaru leaped in front of her, putting up his arm to block the attack. Her jaws clamped on his arm. He grit his teeth as the sharp teeth tore into his flesh.

He had not thought to bring a weapon. At worst he thought they'd be dealing with a traitorous servant. As he wrestled with the monster its strength overpowered him and blood rolled down his arm.

It pushed him backward, almost knocking him off his feet. Hotaru searched the room for some sort of makeshift weapon.

Then a song cut through the chaos. The notes were beautiful, high, and clear. The yokai let go of him, falling backward as it covered its ears screeching. Hotaru turned to see Yuki, her eyes glowing with power, as the entire room vibrated with the energy of her song. The creature turned and fled, breaking through the round window at the back of the room. Hotaru chased after it, watching it scurry across the garden and over a nearby wall.

Yuki's song ended and she was about to collapse when Hotaru rushed to her side and put his arm around her shoulder.

"What was that?" Hotaru asked, looking toward the broken window. He'd never seen anything like it though he'd heard stories of shapeshifters before.

"Get out!" Yuki shouted as she shoved him away.

He turned to look at her, confused.

Tears were rolling down her cheeks.

"I don't think you should be alone. What if that thing comes back?"

"I can handle myself." She shoved him hard, pushing him toward the door. He couldn't make any sense of her reaction. Maybe she didn't want him to see her cry. But he did not press her.

She slammed the door shut once he was out in the hall. He stared at it, trying to process everything he had seen. So, this was why he needed Yuki. With her power, Lord Fujikawa wouldn't stand a chance. With Yuki by his side he would be the most powerful leader of all. With that mystery solved he uncovered another. Why had she pushed him away? What had he done to upset her? It seemed like any time they made progress, they took another two steps back.

He should leave her be but with the thought of that thing coming back through that open window and hurting her, he wouldn't be able to rest.

He knocked on the door. "Yuki. Can you tell me what I did?"

There was no reply.

"I don't know how I upset you."

Silence.

"Answer me or I'm coming in."

Again there was no response. He pushed open the door and rushed in and found it empty. There wasn't a sign of a struggle. It was as if she had vanished into thin air.

There was only one place she could have gone. He climbed through the window, and over the garden wall. Much slower than that monster had. Once he was over the wall, he came face to face with the nighttime forest. It was even more terrifying in the dark. Yuki didn't have much of a head start, so he ran after her.

He wasn't sure what led him to the tree, but it was as if the forest had brought him there. The large oak looked ominous in the night. And Yuki sat against its trunk, looking like a ghost from some fairy tale.

"Go away," she said as he approached.

He stood a few feet away. "Your brother doesn't want you out of the palace," he said, as if that was the only reason he'd come out here. Why had he come here? She hated him, and yet he couldn't stand the idea of her being this miserable or in danger.

She ignored him. And her cold silence was worse. He took a step toward her but she turned to face him with fury in her face.

"Don't come near me, or I'll do to you what I did to that yokai."

Hotaru froze, blinking at her. "I'm not afraid of you, Yuki." He kept his voice low, and calm.

"Of course you are. I saw your face when I banished that creature. You were terrified."

He laughed. Is that what this was about?

"Why are you laughing. Do you think this is funny?"

He stifled his laughter. "This whole time I thought you hated me for being weak. When that thing attacked, you knew just what to do. I am in awe of you. What scared me was that I thought I couldn't protect you."

She stared at him through the gloom of the night. Then very slowly she jumped down to stand in front of him.

"I don't need protection; I'm not like other girls."

"That's what I like about you."

She shook her head. "Don't do that. I know why you really came here."

He froze. She couldn't know what he wanted her for. Could she? His desires for fame and glory hadn't driven him into the forest. It wasn't about that anymore. He had genuinely come to care about her.

"I came because I was worried about you, Yuki."

"Don't lie. My own family thinks I'm a freak. I'm not even human." She crossed her arms over her chest, looking away from him.

He grabbed onto her shoulders and she turned to meet his gaze. "I don't think what you can do makes you less than human."

"You're just saying that."

He held onto her even as she tried to pull away. "My brother is like you. He could see things others could not see his entire life. He tried to hide it and even I condemned him for it."

She was staring up at him, her large eyes reflecting pools of moonlight. "But?"

"I realized how special he was. How lucky he was to have that. It's a gift and you should embrace it."

She turned to look away from him, but he grabbed onto her chin and turned her to face him.

"You are the most beautiful, strong woman I have ever met. I wish I could be a man worthy of you."

She stared up at him for a moment, her eyes tracing over his face. He thought about kissing her but he knew that would ruin this perfect moment and he held back. She turned away from him.

"Come with me. There's something I want to show you."

They traveled deeper and deeper into the forest. Even the sky overhead was blocked by a thick canopy of trees. Hotaru could not see in the dark, but it seemed Yuki could see even in the pitch black. She held his hand, guiding him around obstacles. Then they arrived at a pool. The trees broke away and a shaft of moonlight illuminated the surface of the water, and blue light reflected over everything. Strange lights danced over the water. At first, he thought they were fireflies but their color was all wrong: it was the most vibrant blue, and their dance was nothing like an insect.

In the center of the pool was a small island, and atop it was a simple stone shrine. Yuki sat at the edge of the water and bowed her head, clasping her hands together in prayer. Hotaru joined her in paying respects to the kami who dwelt there. There was an energy to this place, as if all of it was alive and watching.

"I should have died with my mother," Yuki said quietly, her head still bowed.

Hotaru watched her as she spoke, her profile lined in blue light.

"I was very weak when I was born. The midwife did not think I would last through the night. With her dying breath, my mother begged my father to bring me here, to dedicate me to the kami."

She looked up at the statue. The flickering lights had started to gather around the statue, moving in a spiral around it. "In exchange for my life, a part of the kami lives in me. And because of that, I can feel the forest. I can see yokai like most humans cannot. And I have powers others do not."

He bowed his head once more to shrine. "Thank you for saving her."

There was no answer but the wind rustled through the trees overhead. Yuki lifted her head as if listening to something only she could hear. Hotaru looked toward the statue in the center. He thought from the corner of his eye he had seen someone there but when he looked again there was nothing.

19

The kami sat on top of the shrine. His pure white robes rippled around him, floating on the air, though there was no breeze. His long ebony hair was half tied up into a top knot, and rest cascaded over his shoulders, touching the ground. It was impossible to describe his face, because it was that of the divine. Impossibly beautiful and glowing with an inner light of his pure energy. He so rarely showed his face to Yuki, though she always felt him inside her. Looking at him stole her breath away.

"I did not give you life for you not to live, Yuki," he said. "You are not bound to this place as you would believe."

There was no excuse she could give him. None that wouldn't sound selfish and hollow. She didn't want to leave because this place was all she had ever known; this forest was familiar to her. This was where she belonged.

The guardian turned to look at Hotaru. "He is a good man with a good heart. If you were to let him in you would find the happiness that has eluded you."

"You cannot say what will make me happy," Yuki said.

Hotaru, to her left, looked confused. "I never said anything."

"Your mother would not have wanted this for you," the kami said.

"Don't speak of her to me," she snapped.

"What are you talking about?" Hotaru asked.

The guardian's beautiful face was filled with grief.

"Think about what I have said, Yuki, before it's too late," the guardian said as his form slowly dissolved into a thousand twinkling blue lights. And like that he was gone.

"You can't do this to me!" Yuki shouted, wading ankle deep into the pool. "Don't pretend like you care. Where were you when my father died?"

Before she could go any deeper Hotaru grabbed her by the arm, pulling her backward.

"Yuki, who are you talking to?"

The peaceful air of the place was disrupted by her own anger. Once the kami was gone, the place felt darker as a result. Hot tears stung the back of her eyes but she didn't let them fall.

"It was the kami, the deity who protects this forest and my family." She looked up at Hotaru and turned her back on the shrine.

"What did he say?"

She had thought him arrogant and spoiled before, but there was such kindness in him. He was handsome and daring, funny, everything she could have wanted if she'd ever considered such a thing before.

But what she feared more than anything was being caged. To never feel the touch of the guardian again, never look upon his ethereal face. To never run wild. A lord's wife was expected to serve, to look beautiful, to bear children, to obey. That was a life she'd never wanted for herself. And for all his kindness, and no matter how much he made her heart race, if she were to marry him she'd be bound by those same rules.

This was where she belonged. The guardian was wrong, nothing was missing from her.

"Nothing important."

She turned to walk away from the glen. It was foolish to bring Hotaru here. What had she been thinking? Hotaru caught up with her quickly, grabbing her by the shoulder.

"You said, 'this is where I belong.' That sounds important to me."

She glared at him. "Do you think he told me to leave with you? Get married and have a brood of children?"

"Not at all, but clearly something has upset you."

She turned away from him. "What does it matter to you?"

They glared at one another. Her words had hurt him, she could see that clearly. She couldn't stand to look at him another moment and know she'd caused it. She marched through the forest, and Hotaru followed after her not speaking.

It was several minutes before he said, "That monster is still out there. What are you planning on doing?"

It was a relief not only to have a change of subject, but to know he trusted her enough to take care of the problem. "I have to lure it out," she said.

She would root it out like a rat and she would exterminate it.

"I want to help."

She stared at him for a moment, seriously considering his offer. It would be nice to have someone to rely on, but she equally feared trusting him too much would only make their parting that much worse.

"I don't need your help."

She ran from him before he could try and stop her. She was going to have to keep her guard up if she were going to avoid falling into his spell. She returned to the palace, sneaking over the wall that she had escaped from. She'd dealt with this type of yokai before. It fed off human energy. It may have retreated but it wouldn't be far. Spreading out her senses, she felt its energy skulking around the kitchens. It had been taking the form of a maid, and Yuki had been so distracted by Hotaru she hadn't noticed all the signs. It was just another reason to keep him at arm's length. Her negligence had put the clan in danger.

The song that would rend the creature apart, piece by piece, burned inside her. She crept into the kitchen. The cooking fires had burned low but the faint smell of spices still remained.

As Yuki crept across the space, she lost track of the yokai. Its energy disappeared. She spun around, just as it lunged toward her from the dark. A tentacle wrapped around her neck, strangling her throat and preventing her from using her song.

Yuki wrestled the monster, clawing at the tentacle around her throat as it lifted her up into the air, her legs kicking.

"Oh, what a meal you will make." The creature hissed, unhinging its jaw and revealing rows of jagged teeth as it brought her toward its mouth.

Then a blade sliced through the tentacle and Yuki fell to the ground where she gasped for breath and massaged her damaged windpipe.

Hotaru reached for her, a bloody sword in his hand. The creature hissed in his direction before slithering over toward him. One tentacle knocked his weapon out of his hand, while a second wrapped around his body, squeezing the air from his lungs.

Hotaru wrestled against it, holding the tentacles back. But it grabbed onto him and slammed him against a wall where he lost consciousness.

"Hotaru!" she shouted.

As the creature turned its attention back on Yuki, the song of binding poured out of her, burning her throat in its haste to do its work. The creature hissed and tried to fight against her song, its tentacles writhing above its head. But it was no use. Yuki was much stronger. The power wove around her until there was nothing left but a smoking crater on the ground and a single stone in which it had been sealed.

Once the creature was defeated, she rushed to Hotaru's side.

There was a gash on his head, but otherwise there didn't appear to be any broken bones.

"Hotaru, wake up." She shook him gently.

His eyes flicked open and he groaned. "I'm fine." He tried to sit up but stopped mid-way, clutching his head.

"What were you thinking, you idiot?" she chastised. She wanted to strangle him and hug him in equal amounts.

"That I wanted to be a hero," he said as he rubbed his head.

She laughed and rested her head against his shoulder. He was going to be fine if he could joke around.

"Yuki?" he said cautiously. She met his gaze and in the heat of the moment she lost all sense of herself. When he leaned forward and kissed her she didn't fight it. His lips were warm and inviting and a million different sensations were burning up inside her.

It took her a moment to realize what she had done. She pulled back, blinking at him.

"Well. I—I got to go." She leaped up and ran out of the room, her heart hammering more than it had been when she'd been fighting the yokai.

20

Lord Fujimori was propped up like a doll. His stepmother seated just behind him, Yuki on his other side. On the surface, it was a show of household solidarity, in reality, it was likely so someone would be there to catch him were he to collapse. The entire household lined the room.

Hotaru knelt on the ground before him, his head bowed in contrition, but he wasn't here to apologize. Yuki had just finished explaining the yokai to the clan. And deadly silence filled the room. Now all Hotaru had to do was wait for Lord Fujimori's decision.

Lord Fujimori hadn't said a word since Yuki finished. Hotaru kept his head bowed but stole a peek at Yuki. She'd been avoiding him since their kiss. Not that he was that surprised. Even now her eyes were directed away from him, and there was a faint blush on her cheeks.

At last lord Fujimori spoke, "This is a very strange case indeed." His words rolled over the crowd. "We who live within the forest have witnessed these things before. We are fortunate Lord Kaedemori was here and rid us of this menace."

Hotaru's head shot up and looked Lord Fujimori in the eye. He hadn't done anything. He'd been lucky he hadn't gotten himself killed.

Yuki did not protest, instead kept her head lowered.

"I did nothing, Lord Kaedemori. It was Yuki—"

"Nonetheless—" Lord Fujimori cut him off. "We can proceed with the union of our two clans. The wedding will be held in a few weeks' time."

Hotaru's stomach sank. He hadn't told Yuki about their deal. Between their investigation and the attack, there hadn't been a good moment.

Yuki glared at him. She stood up and was preparing to make a scene when Lord Kaedemori began to cough violently, doubling over and clutching his sides. Yuki went to console her brother, but her stepmother was already there, her hand around his shoulder and guiding him out of the room as he coughed.

The crowd murmured as Lord Fujimori was led out of the room, leaving Yuki staring after him. He had to talk to her now, explain everything. But Lord Fujimori on his way out the door, collapsed onto the ground.

The entire audience hall erupted in chaos. Yuki ran to her brother's side. Hotaru chased after her.

"Riku!" Yuki shouted. "Call the healer." She turned and saw Hotaru hovering over her.

Instead of sending him away, she pleaded at him with her eyes and Hotaru went to work.

"Send for the healer." He shouted to a nearby clansman. Then to another. "Help me carry him to his chamber."

Hotaru and another man gently carried the unconscious Lord Fujimori, while Yuki walked beside them holding her brother's hand. They laid him down in his bed just as the healer arrived. He checked his pulse and pressed his hand against his forehead.

"He's going to need rest. All we can do now is wait," the healer said.

Yuki was trembling like a leaf. The crowd and the stress were getting to her. She needed fresh air. Hotaru took her hand and gently led her out of the room into the garden beyond. They were still within earshot if they were needed, but at least they weren't surrounded anymore.

As soon as she was outside Yuki took a few calming breaths and her shaking subsided.

"He's going to be alright. You heard the healer," Hotaru said. He still hadn't let go of her hand.

Yuki shook her head. "It's not going to be alright." She pulled away from him and paced over to a nearby tree, pressing her palm against it. "He's dying just like my father."

"What makes you say that?"

Yuki let out a shaking breath. "It's a curse."

"What do you mean a curse?"

She turned to him, tears in her eyes. "My father had the same symptoms. We consulted every healer we could find. Riku went to every territory, to the most skilled healers. I begged the forest guardian for help. But there's nothing that can stop it. Whatever it is, it consumes them from the inside. And now my brother is dying of the same illness."

He grabbed a hold of her, pressing her against his chest. There was nothing else he could do for her. She clung onto his clothes, tears silently sliding down her face.

"When he's gone, I'll be all alone."

No, you won't. Whatever comes, I will be there for you. Even if I must watch from a distance. I will find a way to keep you safe and happy.

Though he wanted more than anything to speak those words to her, he couldn't make them pass his lips. He was afraid she would push him away. Later when she was calm, he would tell her the truth. But not yet, not now.

Hotaru was just finishing up a letter to home. Lord Fujikawa was moving fast, and if he wanted to beat him he'd need to move quickly. But he couldn't leave Yuki now in the midst of a crisis. There was a knock on the door and he put aside his papers to go and answer it. He opened it to find Lady Fujimori standing outside. Her gaze was lowered.

"What do I owe the pleasure?"

"May I come in?"

It wasn't entirely appropriate. But she lifted her gaze to him, her eyes mesmerizing him. The hairs on the back of his neck stood on end. But despite all his instinct telling him to refuse, he stepped aside to let her in.

She walked into the room, her eyes skimming over his bed, and then turning to him with a smirk. Involuntarily he felt a stirring of lust. He pushed down the feeling. He was officially engaged to Yuki now. He couldn't risk any scandal. And besides he didn't want to hurt Yuki.

"How can I help you, my lady?"

The smile was wiped from her face and she covered her mouth to hide her tears. "I came to you because I didn't know where else to turn."

"What is it?" He took a step toward her, reaching out to take hold of her and comfort her the way he had held Yuki earlier. But it felt wrong and he pulled back.

"My son, Lord Fujimori is dying." She choked on a sob and came forward to grab a hold of his haori, burying her face in it.

Hotaru's gut clenched. Did Yuki know? Was she there with her brother? He should go and comfort her. He'd only left her long enough to write to home. But perhaps Lord Fujimori's condition had worsened since then.

He placed his hands on the lady's shoulders. "I need to go to Yuki."

But as he tried to pull away, her grip tightened. She looked up into his eyes. "Don't go. I don't think I can be alone right now."

As he looked deeper into her eyes, he found himself drowning in her gaze and burning up with a sudden heat that stirred from deep within him. Her cherry-red lips were parted ever so slightly, and tantalizingly close. But even as he dipped in closer to her, Yuki's face popped into his mind.

He gently pushed Lady Fujimori away.

"I can't. I'm sorry. You're beautiful, but there is someone else I love."

"Do you really think she can learn to love you?"

He turned to look at her, his brows shooting to his hairline. "I do."

She smirked slightly. "Even when she finds out why you want to marry her?"

"I've been clear about my motives from the beginning."

"Not all of them."

"I don't know what you're talking about. But I think it's time you left, my lady." He walked to the door, opening it for her. She sauntered toward it, but before she left she rested her hand on his forearm.

"Tell her the truth and see how loyal she remains."

She left Hotaru, and he was left with a slight buzzing in his head as if he'd just had too much to drink.

21

Riku had not risen from his bed for three days. Yuki sat by his bedside tending to him. She watched his shallow breaths and his sunken body shriveling away to nothing. She felt just as powerless as she had when her father died.

She stroked his fevered brow. There were already rumors around the palace. Dissent was growing stronger. It started when Riku showed the first signs of the illness and it was growing louder all the time.

They needed a strong leader. But her brother had no heir. Riku told Yuki her child would rule once he was gone. She wasn't even married. Riku had assumed she'd chosen to marry Hotaru because she'd defended him. And she had to admit she was grateful to have him to lean on during this difficult time. But could she marry him? Since the inception of the clan, her line had ruled. Her father had no brothers, any cousins she had were distant at best. No one had a good claim to rule. If her brother died, it would be chaos. Unless she could take control.

"What should I do, brother?" She stroked his fever brow with a cloth.

Her stepmother came in carrying a tea tray and she set it down beside Yuki. "You look exhausted," she said.

Yuki blinked the exhaustion from her gaze. "I can't leave him."

"Get some rest. I'll watch over him."

She was bone tired but she was afraid if she left his side, he would slip away while she was gone.

"No, I'll stay a while longer."

Not long after that, her head started to bob as exhaustion got its hooks into her. She was forced to take her stepmother's advice and get some rest. But only after getting the promise that her stepmother would wake her at the slightest change in his condition.

She had her futon brought to his room, and she slept close to him just in case she was needed. Her sleep was fitful, full of odd images and at one point she dreamed she was in Hotaru's arms. She woke up drenched in sweat. She crawled over to Riku and watched the steady rise and fall of his chest.

The room was stuffy, kept warm by multiple braziers. Her stepmother was seated by his bedside, just as she had been with her father. She checked his temperature and changed a cold cloth on his forehead. She was a natural and nurturing. All that Yuki was doing was getting in the way.

"You're drenched in sweat, why not get some air?" her stepmother suggested.

Yuki frowned at her. "I don't want to leave him."

"I will send for you. You're not doing anything for him as you are."

Her words stung, but Yuki took her advice and went out to cool her head. The night air was refreshing on her skin, and breathing in the scent of the forest did help to rejuvenate her. Yuki stretched and stared up at the quarter moon.

As she did, she overheard some of her cousins talking.

"We've made multiple appeals, but he will not budge. He has declared Yuki's son his successor."

"The girl is unwed. It is a farce to make a woman elder," replied another.

"But if she were to marry Lord Kaedemori..."

Yuki came around the corner glaring at her cousins.

"How dare you speak of him, my brother is still your lord."

"We've seen how this played out before. For the good of the clan, a strong ruler must be secured."

She bristled at the insinuation. "I would rule just as fairly as my brother and father before me."

"We will never bow to a woman, especially not a witch," they snarled back at her.

In anger, Yuki shoved them. It only agitated them further, and shoving degenerated into a skirmish in the halls. Other family members came and broke apart the fight, while Hotaru grabbed onto her, pinning her arms to her side.

"Your brother and father tried to hide it, but we know. And once he is dead, you will no longer be welcome here!" said one of the men who was being held back.

"Leave now! Before I teach you how to properly address a lady the hard way," Hotaru snarled at them.

They scampered away like scared dogs. Yuki broke herself from Hotaru's embrace.

"I don't need you to fight my battles for me."

"I was trying to protect you from yourself."

She scowled at him. A woman ruler was unheard of; she knew that. And the clan members only tolerated her. She knew that too. But it still stung to hear it.

"I don't need you to do that either." She stalked away from him. Her anger forced her to put distance between herself and her problems. She ran down the hall and toward the garden and climbed the tree out into the forest beyond. She ran, and ran, until her legs burned with exertion and her lungs seized.

When she couldn't run anymore, she found herself at the edge of the forest pool. The only place she could think to go to solve all her problems. She knelt beside it and offered up her prayer. *Please save my brother's life. I'll do anything if you just spare him.*

But as when she came and prayed the same for her father's life, the guardian did not answer. As usual he appeared only when it suited him. But still she remained kneeling by the pool, hoping for a miracle.

"I'll marry Hotaru if that's what it takes!" she shouted, slapping her hand into the mud at the water's edge.

The wind rustled through the trees but there was no answer. Yuki clawed her hand into the mud, making a fist.

If she could take the life from her breast to save his, she would. Her brother was a good man, a good leader, and more deserving of life than her. Why had the guardian saved her life, if he would save no one she loved? Was this the price, to be robbed of happiness?

A twig snapped as footsteps approached behind her. She stood up to see Hotaru standing at the edge of the glen. Had he heard what she offered to the forest guardian?

"How did I know I'd find you here?" He gave her the ghost of a smile.

She crossed her arms over her chest. She hated being exposed in such a way in front of him.

"Why did you follow me?"

"I was concerned about you."

"What do I matter to you?"

Tears rolled down her cheeks. She hadn't even realized they were there until he was wiping them away for her. She grabbed his wrist, and held it when he tried to pull away.

"I would give anything to take this pain away." He pulled her into his arms and enveloped her in his embrace. She let go of all the pain and grief she'd been holding onto.

He stroked her hair and said, "My own family went through a similar unrest. I want to guide you, but I do not want to overstep my bounds."

She clung to his haori, holding onto him, to feel something real and in the flesh. If she married him, it could save her family. But it also meant putting herself in a cage. *I cannot save my brother, but maybe I can save the clan.* As an experiment, she leaned forward and kissed him. She meant for it to just be a peck on the lips, just to see if it felt as magical as the first time. But as soon as she did, he pulled her in closer and his arms wrapped around her. At first, she tensed, but then very gently, he parted her lips with his tongue. And it was as if everything but the feel of his body next to hers melted their surroundings. She was lost in him. In the feeling of his arms around her, of the taste on his lips. There was nothing in the world but the two of them.

They broke apart, panting for breath.

He took a step back. "I'm sorry. I shouldn't have."

But she grabbed him and kissed him again. It was just as earth-shattering.

"I wanted you to," she said.

He leaned his forehead against hers. "What are you doing to me?" He exhaled.

She laughed. "What are you doing to me?" She'd never felt like this before, never felt like she was willing to give everything up for someone. It wasn't just to save the clan, she couldn't stand the idea of letting him go.

She didn't dare speak the words that were on her heart. But she thought she felt the brush of the guardian's presence. When she looked up there was nothing there, but Hotaru was staring at the place she'd last seen him.

22

The guardian revealed himself shimmering and translucent. He spoke to Hotaru not so much in words, but a feeling. The message he tried to relay was unclear but he was certain it had something to do with Yuki. She needed him.

"What is it? What do you see?" Yuki touched his shoulder.

Hotaru blinked and looked away from the guardian back to Yuki. The same ethereal glow he'd seen around the guardian illuminated Yuki as well. There was no doubt the two were tied together.

"I think he was trying to warn me of something."

"What?"

"If your brother dies without a clear successor it will become a bloodbath."

She flinched. "I have a plan. I'm going to convince them to let me rule."

"Talking won't be enough. You've seen how they feel."

She balled her hands into fists at her side. "Do you not think I can handle this on my own?"

He hated to ruin their moment, but this was urgent. He'd seen the chaos that ensued when he'd taken control of the clan from

Hikaru. Even with a strong hand to guide them, there had been hiccups. He wouldn't be embroiled in this war otherwise.

"You've seen how they reacted to the idea of you as an elder. But your brother made your child successor. If you had a husband—"

"How convenient. Isn't this what you wanted all along?"

He took a step toward her and she didn't run away this time. He wouldn't force her. "The choice is yours. If you tell me to walk away right now and never come back, I will. I am yours to command."

She searched his face. "You say that now, but the moment we're married I become a pretty doll used to entertain, locked away in a cage."

He cupped her cheek. "That's not what you would be to me."

"You swore you'd never bring this up again." She didn't sound nearly as angry as before.

"But this is different."

She looked away from him, back toward the palace, where her cousins and clansmen were likely tearing one another apart for the chance to rule. If only she'd felt or seen what the guardian had shown him. She needed him, and what other way could he help than this?

"I don't know," she said.

"It would be in name only. I won't ask anything of you in return. You can remain here and be free."

She pulled away from him, putting a gap between them that he knew he could not breach. She crossed her arms over her chest and turned away from him.

"Give me time to think about it."

They returned to the palace together. Yuki scaled the palace wall, and Hotaru followed after her. But as soon as he was over the wall, he felt it on the air. Like the buzz of insects. She must have sensed it too, and ran ahead without a word. Hotaru followed after her toward the audience hall. There they found the household in chaos. It appeared a gathering had been underway but it had degraded into an all-out brawl. Some men wrestled on the floor, while others were shouting at one another, their faces turning purple.

Yuki dived into the fray, ducking between squabbling clansmen and weaving around others who were wrestling on the ground. Hotaru attempted to follow her, but one man dodged a punch that then came toward him. He took a blow to the jaw and stumbled backward. Hotaru came back and knocked the other man flat on his back. By the time he disentangled himself from the fight, Yuki was at the front of the room. She whistled to get everyone's attention. The shrill noise worked like a bucket of water poured over the crowd.

Everyone in the room turned toward her. "Why are you fighting? Now more than ever we should be unified!" Her voice carried over the room, filled with authority and power.

The bright light he'd noticed in the guardian's glen shone from within her. She was beautiful and fierce, and he realized he would follow her to the ends of the earth if she asked him.

"This is no concern for a woman!" one of the clansmen shouted.

"I know you are all afraid for the future. But we have been through worse before," Yuki replied, her arms outstretched.

"Who will lead us?" shouted another man from the back.

Yuki jutted out her chin and stared across the room. For a moment her eyes met his and he felt a jolt roll through him. He nodded his head, giving her what support he could from a distance. This was her choice.

"I will lead you," Yuki said.

It felt as if the air had been sucked out of the room. Then the men all roared, rushing forward. But the consensus was clear, they would not take a woman's rule. Yuki needed him. Hotaru elbowed his way through to the front. Even as they pressed in around her, calling her horrible slurs, she did not back down.

One man reached her, trying to grab her, and she flipped him onto his back, just as she had done to him. It didn't deter the mob, and instead more men reached for her. Hotaru got to the front, punching a man who was pulling at Yuki's haori.

"Stand down!" he shouted, putting himself in front of Yuki.

The men glared and jeered at him but did not come any closer.

"This does not concern you, outsider," a man closest to him snarled.

"I will not let you harm her."

"She's not a woman but a beast!" Another man shouted from the back.

Yuki growled and lunged forward but Hotaru held out his arm to keep her back.

"She is Lord Fujimori's chosen heir, and you should all be bowing to her."

"We will not be ruled by a woman!" someone said.

"You know Yuki, you know she could beat any of you here in a fair fight. She could rule just as well as any man, perhaps better."

They only grumbled and shouted. "She can rule if she has a husband," came one of the elder's replies.

There was more grumbling but less violent than before.

He did not turn to look at her, but he felt her stare from his side. He wanted to give her the choice, but he couldn't put her in danger. They'd never accept her alone. This was the only way he could protect her. Hotaru took a deep breath.

"I am going to marry Yuki. It was decided by Lord Fujimori and me before he fell ill."

He felt Yuki's stare on the side of his head. He should have told her sooner, but it was too late now.

"Why should we trust you?" asked an old man near the front.

"Because you need a strong leader in the coming days. Lord Fujikawa is gathering an army. He is coming this way. Either you join me and keep your own family in power, or let him destroy everything you hold dear."

There was more rumbling and a lot more back and forth. It took hours of deliberation and a vote among the elders. But then it was decided, Hotaru would be the new elder once he married Yuki and Lord Fujimori passed. Hotaru had been so absorbed in settling the clan business, he had not even noticed Yuki slipping out.

He went in search of her and found her in the garden.

"There you are. I was looking for you."

Her glare threatened to melt him into a puddle. He'd been expecting this.

"I'm sorry I didn't say anything sooner. I wanted to let you decide, but I couldn't think of any other way to protect you."

He reached for her, but she knocked his hand away. "I told you. I don't need you to save me." Would it hurt her to thank him? They were about to tear her apart. This had to be what the guardian was trying to tell him, Yuki needed him. Even if she couldn't accept his love. He could do this much to protect her.

"You do need me."

She turned around to slap him but he caught her wrist.

"You lied to me. I was a fool to trust you." She yanked her hand away and stormed down the hall. He didn't try to chase her, it was too late for that.

23

As much as it pained her to think about marrying for convenience, giving up her freedom could secure her father's legacy and fulfill her brother's dying wish. But marrying Hotaru? She'd been an idiot to think it was ever her choice. He said he would give her wings, but this was a cage. He couldn't be trusted. He'd lied to her at every turn. The very idea clawed at her throat and made it difficult to breathe.

She paced the length of her brother's room. He had made no improvement, and while she should be tending to him, instead she was letting thoughts of Hotaru consume her. The tanuki had come looking for her. Since she hadn't been in the forest in a while, they were worried. They sat lined up along the route she paced, watching her walk back and forth. Their heads bobbed with the rhythm of her steps.

"I can't marry him," she said as she went one direction. And then as she turned and walked the other direction, "I can't let the clan fall apart either."

The tanuki had no advice. They were much better at playing tricks than making life-altering decisions. Happi leaped up and followed after her as she stalked back and forth, quickly followed by his brothers.

She was completely absorbed in her pacing until her brother wheezed and gasped for breath. Yuki froze, her eyes pinned on Riku, waiting for him to inhale once more. It was several painful seconds before he took a breath. Only then did Yuki exhale. The tanuki, unprepared for her abrupt halt, collided with the back of her legs.

They squabbled with one another for a moment until Yuki settled their arguments and gave them a shiny hairpin to play with. She knelt down beside her brother's bed, staring at his gaunt face. He'd grown thin in the preceding month. Now he looked almost skeletal. She replaced the rag on his forehead with a fresh one.

"Brother, what do I choose?" she asked his sleeping form, but there was no answer.

She leaned her head on his chest, listening to the gentle rise and fall of his breathing. How much longer could she cling onto his dying body? Just like her father before him, her brother would not recover. It was up to her to keep the family together. She had no choice.

The door to the room opened and the tanuki quickly turned into inanimate objects as to not be seen. Yuki turned to see her stepmother walking in with a cup of tea.

"How is he?" she asked as she came in and handed Yuki a cup. She held it in her hand, letting the warmth seep into her.

"The same," Yuki replied tersely. It wasn't her stepmother's fault that he was ill of course. But she hated how she continued to hover over him, pushing Yuki away. It was her responsibility to take care of Riku, not some outsider.

"You've been by his side every moment. Don't you want to rest?"

"No."

"Well, drink your tea at least."

Yuki stared it for a moment, thinking of refusing out of petty spite. Riku wouldn't have liked it if she did. He wanted them to be a family. She took the cup and brought it to her lips, but before she took a sip, she lowered it.

She'd never gone to her stepmother for advice, but if Riku died she really would be all that was left of Yuki's family and she hardly knew anything about the woman.

"Why did you marry my father?" Yuki asked.

Her stepmother smiled slightly and then looked away, probably embarrassed. "What a strange question."

For so long, she'd pushed her away. Maybe she could give her a chance. "Did you love him?"

Her stepmother looked at her. There was a strange glint in her eye. It made her uneasy. The hairs on Yuki's neck prickled.

"Why do you ask?" her stepmother said.

Yuki rolled the teacup between her hands. "If Riku dies, you're the last family I have left. And we've never really gotten along."

She reached across and put her hand on Yuki's. "I know I could never replace your mother."

Yuki swallowed past a lump in her throat. "No, you can't." It had never been about her taking her mother's place. But her stepmother had supplanted her place by her father's side. Everyone said her father spoiled her. They were always together. But when he'd remarried, it was like Yuki didn't exist anymore.

Her stepmother squeezed Yuki's hand. "If you'll let me give you some advice?"

Yuki met her gaze and nodded slowly. She was desperate for guidance.

"You should marry Lord Kaedemori. For your brother's sake and for the good of the clan."

Yuki sighed. She was afraid she'd say that. There was no use running away from it anymore. She set down her tea. "I need to head out, send word if his condition changes?"

Her stepmother nodded. "Of course."

She headed out in search of Hotaru. She found him talking with the elders of the clan. They were all stroking their beards and nodding their heads. As Yuki approached she heard what they were saying.

"With you as leader of the clan, we can feel confident again."

Hotaru bowed to them. "I'm glad I have your support."

As he straightened, he saw the elders staring at her. He turned toward her and his face flushed. "Yuki."

She stifled her anger. This wasn't about the two of them anymore. It was what was best for the clan.

"We need to talk," she said coldly before turning to walk away, hoping he would follow.

It didn't matter if she agreed to this marriage or not. The decision had been made without her. But she wanted to at least keep the illusion of choice. She led him back to the garden where the peach tree was in full bloom. White petals floated on the breeze. Spring was here at last. She avoided looking at him by watching the petals dance on the wind.

"It's not what it looks like—"

"I have no choice but to marry you. But before that happens, I want to make some things clear."

"Yuki, don't be like that." He grabbed her shoulder, but she spun around to face him, hands up to defend herself if need be.

"Don't touch me," she snarled.

His eyes searched her face, pain written there that she didn't want to see. "I meant it when I said it was your choice. I've spoken to the elders and they'll support your rule."

She crossed her arms over her chest. She'd fallen for his lies before. "And what's the catch?"

"We get married and have an heir as soon as possible. Our child would rule over both clans." It felt like a punch to the gut. She'd been deluding herself into thinking he was any different than the ones who came before them.

"I figured as much."

"I'll admit, I came here looking for an alliance. But it's not just that anymore."

"What if you could have me without the alliance?" It was a gamble, and one that would likely shatter her heart to pieces, no matter what his answer.

"If I had the choice we'd leave all this behind."

"But you don't have the choice, right?"

He swallowed hard, his throat bobbing up and down. "What about my people? What happens to them, Yuki? This isn't just about you and me."

"Isn't that the problem? This should only be about you and me. None of these other things would matter if you really loved me."

"We're different. We have responsibilities." He reached for her again and she backed away.

"I know. And that's why I'll marry you. But I will never trust you again."

24

Hotaru was dressed. The clan was waiting. But he couldn't move. He was frozen in place, trapped in his room, terrified of taking a step. The look on Yuki's face haunted him still. He didn't want to marry her, not because he didn't love her. It was quite the opposite actually. Instead of bringing them closer together, this marriage would push her completely out of his reach. He was getting everything he wanted: the support of the Fujimoris and Yuki's control of the clan. And yet he felt hollow. He'd been greedy. He wanted her and the alliance but he couldn't have both.

A hand slid over his chest from behind. He hadn't even heard the door open. He thought he had been alone. He spun around to find the Lady Fujimori smiling at him. There was something about her, that he didn't question why she touched him, or how she'd gotten in without making a sound.

"My lady, is there anything wrong?"

"Everything is fine. I thought you might want something to drink." She offered up a tray with a steaming teacup.

"Thank you," he said.

He took the cup and drained it in one shot while she watched him. When he was finished he placed the teacup onto the tray.

"Is everything prep—" he stopped and clutched his head, a sudden dizziness overcoming him.

"Are you alright?" she asked, grabbing onto his arm. "You should sit."

Hotaru sat down, and as the room swayed around him Lady Fujimori knelt in front of him. She placed both hands on his biceps, and her gaze filled his vision.

"The wedding. I need to get going." His words were muddled as slow, his thoughts in a fog.

Her hands glided down his arms, then across his torso going lower and lower. Before she could reach into his hakama, he stilled her roaming hands by grabbing her wrists.

"I'm about to marry your daughter," he said as he shook his head. But that proved to be a mistake because the room spun even more.

She smiled up at him and pretended to smooth a spot on his pants, her hands gliding too close to his manhood.

"There's time yet," she said.

Lady Fujimori leaned forward and brushed her hand against his neck. As she did, he felt a prick. He hissed in response and touched the spot which throbbed. When he pulled back his hand there was blood on it.

"Oh no, I scratched you." She pulled back, his blood like a crimson flower on the tip of her pointed fingernail. Had they always been that long and sharp? He couldn't remember.

"No, it's nothing."

His vision blurred and she came in and out of focus. Before he knew it, he was lying on the ground, and the woman was straddling him. She cupped his face in her hands, leaning downward to give him a kiss.

He couldn't fight it. In fact, he found his body reacting despite his mind's protests. She leaned back with a smile.

"You're stronger than the rest. Hopefully you'll last longer than them too."

"What did you do to me?" he tried to say, but his words came out more slurred and incoherent than before and sounded more like a pained groan.

"Shh, my darling, don't worry about that now. We'll be together soon, after your wedding night."

"No," he moaned.

"Tonight you are going to kill Yuki with this knife." She placed the knife in his hand and his fingers obediently curled around it.

He wanted to protest but he couldn't make his body obey his commands. She dipped her head down to kiss him once more and then everything went black.

Hotaru woke to a startled servant who'd found him lying unconscious on the floor. "My lord, is everything alright?"

Hotaru's head was pounding but he could not remember how he had ended up on the ground. The last thing he remembered was getting dressed for the wedding.

The servant helped him to his feet. His head felt a bit foggy but other than that he was fine. "Has the ceremony started?"

"The ceremony is about to start, but if you are unwell perhaps we should delay it—"

"No! We must get married." This alliance was riding on this wedding. It couldn't be canceled. He'd find a way to sway Yuki. He'd convinced her to marry him, hadn't he?

The servant looked skeptical but did not argue. After dusting off his clothes, they hurried out toward the palace shrine where the wedding was to be held. The household had already gathered as Hotaru took his place.

A divider separated him from Yuki, but he still tried to catch a peek between the slats of wood. Until they stood before the altar together, he would not see her. The presiding priestess chanted and rang the ceremonial bells as Hotaru took a step forward. His heart hammered in his chest.

For good or ill, there was no stopping it now. The divider ended and Yuki walked in place beside him, nothing but a blur of white. More than anything he wanted to gaze upon her, but he feared seeing the hatred in her eyes as well and held back.

They both knelt before the priestess. Hotaru lifted his gaze to see the witch smiling at him. This was what she had wanted after all. He should be happy as well, everything was going as he had planned it. He chanced a glance at Yuki, but her wide hood hid her face and she kept her gaze forward. He turned away. They could talk after the ceremony.

The kami's blessing was invoked by the witch, and then the pair took drinks from the sacred sake, while the priestess continued her liturgy of blessings upon them: for fertility, for long life, and for happiness. Then they were purified with the water sprinkled on them by the branch of a holy tree. They spoke their own vows, and there was a slight tremor in Yuki's voice as she gave hers. Otherwise the ceremony went on without incident. The houses of Kaedemori and Fujimori were forever united.

After the wedding ceremony they were presented to the clan, who roared with approval. At least someone was happy. Hotaru tried catching Yuki's eye once more, but she continued to avoid his gaze. Even as the family feasted in celebration, they sat side by side in complete silence. At the end of the meal, they were escorted to their bedroom where they would be expected to consummate their marriage. Yuki could avoid him no longer.

Alone at last, Yuki stood at the farthest end of the room. Her back to him as she looked at the window. Most likely she was contemplating escaping out it.

"Yuki—" he started to say but a sudden pain ripped through his skull. He paused, massaging his head.

"Don't even think about it. I may be your wife but you don't have my body."

"I would never try to force you into anything you didn't want," he said through gritted teeth. The pain in his skull felt enough to rip it open.

"Just like you didn't want to trick me into a marriage."

"If you would let me—ahhh." He cried out, collapsing to his knees. The pain was so intense he couldn't see.

He wrapped his arms around his body and his hand brushed against a knife concealed there. As soon as he touched it, the pain receded. He reached into the folds of his haori and removed it. The pain disappeared completely. *What is this doing here?* He kept it hidden from view.

"Don't try—" she turned and seeing him doubled over on the floor she rushed toward him. "Hotaru, what's wrong?"

He clutched the knife tighter. *Kill her.*

"I won't," he groaned.

"Won't what?"

He drew the knife, but before Yuki could escape he grabbed her by the shoulder, holding in place. She struggled against him.

"What are you doing?"

But he couldn't speak. Couldn't warn her. The knife plunged toward her heart.

25

Yuki turned as the knife came toward her. There was no time to dodge the blow. She threw out her hands, grabbing onto Hotaru's wrist, wrestling against him. The two of them struggled for a moment with the blade between them. Hotaru's superior strength won out and the blade inched toward her.

She tried to wriggle out of his grasp but it was no use, his hold of her was too strong. The blade cut through the layers of her wedding kimono and then stopped, just inches before it pierced her heart. Hotaru's arm shook.

Through gritted teeth he said, "Run."

She broke free of his grip and scrambled backward, but he was standing between her and the door. Yuki scanned the room for a quick escape. The window was not big enough for her to squeeze through, and besides it would leave her back exposed. Hotaru cried out and Yuki whipped her head in his direction as he fell to his knees. The knife was still clutched in his hand as his body trembled. He slammed the knife onto the ground, the flat of his palm resting on top of it. It appeared he was struggling to remove his hand, but some invisible force was keeping him from doing so.

The sensible thing to do would be to run away from him. But she knew Hotaru now. He would never try to harm her. Yuki inched over toward him. His gaze was trained on the ground and his breathing was coming out in painful gasps. As she approached, he growled like a wounded animal. And just like she would a cornered beast, she moved slowly toward him. When she got close, however, he burst up, swinging the knife at her once more.

Yuki dodged to the side and managed to get behind him. She grabbed the hand that held the knife behind his back and forced him to drop it.

"Hotaru, I know this isn't you. I'm going to try and help you."

She'd taken the knife from him, but with his size and strength she was no match for him and he broke free of her hold. Grabbing a hold of her arm, he flipped her onto the ground. Hotaru straddled her and his hands wrapped around her throat. There was no more room for hesitation.

The notes of a song burned through her and slammed into Hotaru's chest. The force of the blow threw him off her and he slammed against a nearby wall. As he tried to rise and attack her again, Yuki sang, letting the power of the forest flow through her. It wove around her, illuminating her in golden light, and wrapped around Hotaru. He threw his head back, screaming in agony as his body contorted from the force of the song.

He fell to his knees once more and bent over retching. A thick black sludge pooled on the ground, staining the tatami. Once he had purged himself of all the thick black liquid, he collapsed onto his side. Yuki panted for breath and sat back to watch him. His face was pale and sweaty, and he remained lying on his side, eyes half closed.

"What happened to me?" he asked. His voice was hoarse.

"You were being controlled by a yokai."

"I was? How is that possible?"

Yuki frowned. If only she could talk to the forest guardian and ask his advice, but there wasn't time. Whoever had been trying to kill her wasn't the yokai they'd destroyed. That had likely been a diversion. There was someone else pulling the strings. And if her hunch were correct, they would be here soon to make sure the job was done.

"They likely don't appear to be yokai, but are pretending to be human. We need to lure them out."

"How?"

"We give them what they want." She smirked.

Hotaru sat up unsteadily. His eyes scanned her face. "I must be the luckiest man in the world."

The sudden intimacy made her uncomfortable, and Yuki stood and crossed the room. The space between them felt charged. She cleared her throat. "Don't get any funny ideas."

He gave her a crooked smile. "Don't worry. I won't."

"Good." But this situation was anything but. She didn't want him to know how scared she'd been to lose him. She didn't want to admit it out loud but she was falling in love with him. To him this was just an alliance.

The room was dark as Hotaru sat on the edge of the futon watching the door. Yuki's immobile body lay just a few feet from him. The fake blood and mangled corpse were enough to give him nightmares, even if he knew it was all the tanuki's illusion. He couldn't look at the fake blood on his hands or the stained clothes.

Footsteps approached outside and he tensed. He stood up before thinking it would be too obvious, but who could sleep next to a corpse? *A man who's possessed.*

Hotaru took a deep breath and laid down on the futon, just moments before the door opened. A shaft of light illuminated the room in a pale-yellow glow before being extinguished when the door closed. Soft footsteps crossed the chamber.

"Wake up, my darling," a soft feminine voice cooed.

Hotaru stretched and sat up, and had to suppress his shock at who had entered the room. Lady Fujimori was holding a tray with steaming tea, her hair unbound and in her night clothes.

She set the tea down beside him before kneeling in front of him. She ran her hands up his legs.

"You've done good work. Now I am all yours." She leaned forward and kissed him on the mouth, and wanting to play along with the charade, he let her. But he felt Yuki's presence like a fire on the back of his skull.

She pulled away and went over to light one of the rooms braziers. She flicked her fingers and the room was filled with light. Yuki's bloody body lay on the ground in front of her, and she smiled.

"I thought you were going to need more tea to make you obedient, but you're a good boy, aren't you?"

"I am," he said in a detached voice. She sauntered closer to him before wrapping her arms around his body, her hands roving lower.

"You shall be a feast. With your energy and virility, you will last much longer than Riku."

She leaned forward to kiss him again and he gave the signal. The tanuki who'd been posing as Yuki's corpse transformed with a pop and a puff of smoke. Lady Fujimori turned and upon realizing she'd been tricked, she transformed.

Her beautiful face contorted into something monstrous. Her cheekbones ended at sharp points and her long black hair turned into writhing tentacles which rose up behind her. They wrapped around Hotaru's body and squeezed.

Just then Yuki burst into the room, carrying a sword.

The yokai turned toward her. "I should have killed you when I had the chance," she hissed.

Yuki lunged toward her, but as she did the yokai knocked her backward, slamming her into the wall. She kept Hotaru lifted into the air where he fought against the tentacles. She stalked closer toward Yuki, who was pinned by the hair tentacles to the wall.

Yuki struggled against her. "You killed my father and you were trying to kill my brother too."

The yokai laughed. "I did. And I'll take your lover as well."

"If I was in the way, why not just kill me?"

The creature hissed. "The forest protected you until you swore yourself to another. Now that protection is gone."

Yuki's eyes grew wide and Hotaru realized what he had done by making her marry. That had been the monster's intention all along. She must have swayed the elders in their favor, forced them together. He pushed against the bindings of the monster's hair but it was no use.

The creature unhinged her jaw, revealing rows of jagged teeth as she stalked closer to Yuki. As she approached Yuki, her eyes started to glow. It was a bright light that was almost blinding. Then a song burst from her lips. The words full of ancient power. The creature shrieked and tried to back away, but there was no use, Yuki's power tore through her until there was nothing left but ashes on the ground.

Hotaru fell with a thump and Yuki rushed over to help him up. "Are you alright?"

"I'm fine, thanks to you." He grinned at her.

She had her hands on his shoulders, and their faces were inches apart. The magic still flickered around her. He felt it like a slight buzz in his ear. She took a step back. Nothing had changed between them. He'd still forced her into this marriage, and by doing so it had put her in danger. There was only one thing he could do for her now.

"I was going to tell you before. But I'm leaving tomorrow."

Her eyes were wide with shock. "What?"

"We have our alliance. You're free to live your life as you wish. I will not trouble you anymore."

They stared at one another, neither of them daring to speak.

But he desperately wanted her to say anything, to give him the slightest sign that he shouldn't go.

"That's for the best then."

He kept his expression neutral, not wanting her to know how those few words struck him like a blow to the gut.

26

The forest pond was cloaked in silence, even the wind did not blow through the trees as Yuki knelt at the edge of the pool. The guardian's shrine in the center was cold and unmoving. There was never any guarantee the guardian would show up. But now more than ever, she needed his guidance.

"Please, I need to know what I should do," she begged.

Her knees were soaked from the wet earth and her back hurt from kneeling this long on the ground. Hotaru was leaving, and she should let him go. He'd only come here for an alliance; he didn't really care for her. But a part of her wanted to ask him to stay. She was in love with him, but she didn't know how to say it.

But as was expected there was no answer. The tanuki, who rarely came to this place, had held a silent vigil while she prayed. But as an entire day passed, she knew there was no answer coming. The decision was up to her. No one could tell her what to do now.

Yuki returned to the palace and to her brother's room. Once the yokai was destroyed, he had woken up and in the days since the yokai's extermination he was beginning to recover.

As Yuki came into his room, he was sitting up in bed, eating with more vigor than she'd seen in a very long time. There was a healthy pink flush to his cheeks.

"Slow down our you're going to get a stomach ache." Yuki laughed as she sat beside his futon.

"You were out in the forest again," he said through a mouthful of food. Grains of rice dribbled onto his chin.

She shook her head and wiped them away. "I was."

He swallowed his food and said, "Did you figure out what you needed to?"

She sighed. "No."

He set aside his empty rice bowl and then took her by the hand. "I never should have pressured you into marrying. If you're very unhappy, we can undo the marriage."

"We cannot undo what has been done. We are bound together by the kami."

"The kami would not want you with a man who nearly killed you. And who knows what else he's capable of?"

"It wasn't Hotaru who tried to kill me, but our stepmother."

Her brother flushed and looked down. Her hooks remained in him. The memory of the woman who had taken care of him could not be erased, even if her spell was broken.

He cleared his throat. "I just want you to be happy, Yuki."

She patted his hand. "I am happy."

"You don't seem like it."

She sighed again. She wasn't sure what she wanted. No matter the reasons, Hotaru had lied to her. But the idea of never seeing Hotaru again clenched at her heart and threatened to tear it to pieces. But she couldn't leave the forest behind, it was her solace and her serenity.

"I will be, don't worry." She forced a smile for Riku's sake.

Yuki went to the garden after that, watching the koi soothed her mind. The tanuki followed her into the garden and hovered around her, playing and splashing in the water. Their antics amused her but it didn't bring her any closer to a decision.

They stopped their playing and froze. She turned to see what they were looking at and saw Hotaru standing at the edge of the garden. He had his hands folded behind his back and he seemed to be muttering to himself as he paced just out of sight. When she looked at him, she knew what her decision was. She had to tell him the truth.

She got up to greet him and as she approached his head shot up.

He walked toward her and they both stopped a few feet away. They were husband and wife, bound together by the kami. But from the distance between them you would have thought they were perfect strangers.

He cleared his throat. "I came to say goodbye."

"Goodbye?" She choked on the word. *Don't let him go, tell him you need him!*

He nodded his head. "We made an agreement, and I plan on upholding my end. Besides, I have a war to deal with."

He trailed off. But Yuki could see it all clearly now: the fear she'd kept hidden all this time, the rejection she knew for certain would always come at his hand.

"Well, I suppose you have no reason to stay now that you have your treaty." She let her own bitterness get the better of her, when all she wanted was to hold onto him and never let him go.

"That's not it—"

"Goodbye, Hotaru." She turned and strode away from him. She didn't want him to see her tears. `

Hotaru left early the next morning. Yuki didn't stop to watch him go. She wasn't going to make a complete fool out of herself in front of the entire clan. She'd been an idiot to think he cared for her at all. Now that he was gone, her life could go back to how it was before.

The days that followed went down a familiar path, her brother's health steadily improved and life at the castle returned to how it was before Hotaru ever arrived. It was as if he had never been there at all. She received a formal letter from Hotaru, which she refused to read but her brother read to her, informing her that Hotaru had arrived home safely. It was over now. But there was a deep ache in her chest that wouldn't go away.

She went to the guardian's spring almost every day, searching for answers to her unasked question. It was quiet and still as usual. When she approached she knelt down to pray. She kept her vigil for hours but there was no response. She got up to leave but an elderly priestess was blocking her way. She had long white hair and a crescent-shaped scar by her eye. No priestess tended this place. No one came here but Yuki.

"Who are you?" Yuki demanded, taking a defensive pose. It could very well be another yokai in disguise.

"Your heart is heavy, child." The holy energy of a priestess exuded from the woman and her words had a calming effect on Yuki.

On closer inspection, Yuki recognized her as the woman who had conducted the marriage ceremony between her and Hotaru. She had remained at the palace since, tending to the palace shrine.

"How did you find this place?" Yuki said, ignoring her comments.

The old woman held up her hand and a flickering blue light that Yuki associated with the guardian landed on her hand. The old woman smiled at it.

"I know a place of power when I see it." The light fluttered away from her and she smiled at Yuki.

"What do you want with this place?" The woman seemed harmless, but she'd been deceived before.

"It is not this place that I seek, but you, child."

"What do you want with me?"

"Your heart has been crying out these past weeks since your husband left."

Yuki placed her hand over her heart.

"I don't know what you're talking about." She brushed past the woman, intending to hide herself in the forest. She hated feeling this exposed, especially to a stranger.

"You want to forget."

She froze in place as tears sprang to her eyes and ran down her cheeks. Yuki wiped away the tears and turned back to the old woman.

"I can help you forget," the old woman said.

It was foolish to even entertain the idea. Nothing came without a price, she knew that. But this pain wouldn't go away and by now she'd give anything to pretend Hotaru had never walked into her life. "How?"

The old woman reached into her sleeves and revealed a golden peach. It was the most perfect and plump peach she'd ever seen in her life. The old woman placed it in Yuki's hands.

"Eat from this peach and when you have finished, you will forget everything that makes your heart ache."

Yuki held the peach in her hand. It trembled with power. Was this the only solution? She wanted her life as it had been. But even if she forgot, it wouldn't erase her marriage.

"I cannot just forget. I am... married."

"All vows you made will be wiped away when you bite from this peach. You will be free."

Yuki's hands shook at that one, bittersweet word—free. Before she could rethink it, she took a bite. And as soon as the juice touched her lips, she felt the power burning up inside her. Rising up and flowing out of her.

"What did you do—" Yuki gasped and clutched at her throat. The golden light of the kami's power poured out of her and into the old woman.

Her body transformed and time reversed itself. She went from a very old woman to a girl Yuki's age, with an uncanny resemblance to her. The last of her power seeped from her and Yuki collapsed onto the ground, the bitten peach rolling from her lifeless fingers.

27

"You've grown desperate," the guardian said. Yuki's crumpled body lay at his feet. As a kami he was often forced to stand outside the happenings of nature, but being a part of her had deepened their connection. But as he was outside the mortal realm, he was powerless to stop the witch.

"It was that child's choice," the witch said with a wicked gleam in her eyes.

"My power will not sustain you long. For something as old as you, I would have thought you would know."

"This is merely a temporary fix. The girl I was grooming as my next body is out of my reach now."

"One of your girls got out of reach?" He threw his head back and laughed. "So that is why you've grown so bold as to risk the wrath of the kami."

The witch shrugged her shoulders. "I do not fear you, forest guardian.

"And what of the punishment of The Eight?"

She laughed. "The Eight left this plain long ago. They will not bother with one girl."

This witch was dangerous. Perhaps it would be better if he spoke to his siblings about returning to earth.

The guardian of the forest only shook his head. Those who craved immortality were the most dangerous. "I can see why you'd want Yuki, by why that man Hotaru?"

"You should understand, guardian. It is good to be worshiped."

She reached down toward Yuki, perhaps to hide her evil deed by disposing of the body, or worse yet, she intended to take her body for her own. That was how this vile creature had lived well beyond a mortal's time. But he could not stand the idea of her taking her. Though his power in the mortal realm was limited, he sent his vines to pick up Yuki's body, encapsulating it, protecting it from the witch by shrouding it with his holy energy.

"You've grown attached to her, have you?"

Cocooned in his vines, the kami felt the faintest flicker of Yuki's soul. She was not gone from this world yet. She was a fighter. But there was little time left.

The witch sang, attempting to undo his protection. When she got close, he unfurled his power toward her in a flash of bright light.

Her song clashed against his holy energy. The fool had thought he was one of the thousand lesser gods. But that was not the case and he deflected her song with ease. He fired her song back at her, burning her face in the process. She turned to hide the damaged skin, which was already knitting itself back together. Her lips curled back in a sneer.

"I will leave you the girl, my gift to you." She threw her head back to laugh. "Lord of the Animals."

She disappeared in the rush of the wind and the guardian, trapped in the world of the divine, could do nothing but cradle Yuki's body. He might not be able to restore the spark of life into her, but he could shield her until someone who could arrived.

He called for the tanuki, the seven brothers who loved Yuki

dearly. They were never far from her, and they approached slowly. Some of them cried loudly at her loss.

"It is not too late," he told them. "The bravest of you must go and find the man, Hotaru. Only he can save her now."

The oldest of them, the one Yuki called Kashikoi, stepped forward. With the little power he had available he gave the tanuki his blessing of protection. He was young yet, and had a very long and dangerous journey ahead of him.

"Go," he commanded.

The tanuki ran into the forest, off in search of her savior. His brothers sat along the shore, preparing for a long vigil. He just hoped the little tanuki could bring Hotaru back before it was too late.

Hotaru stared across his empty room, the wide-open space faced his garden. The winter frost had started to melt away and left thick, muddy slush behind. Trees stripped of all foliage, reached skeletal fingers toward the gray sky. Clouds gathered on the horizon, threatening rain. The clan house felt bleak and inhospitable.

The cultured gardens of home were wastelands and the simpering greetings of his clansmen were hollow. He'd locked himself away in his room. He'd promised Yuki her freedom. He'd never thought doing so would be like carving out a piece of his heart.

War was imminent. One he had pursued for the glory and honor of his house. But as Hotaru sat down on the edge of his futon, and dropped his head into his hands, he wondered if the fame was worth it. When he'd taken control over the clan, he aspired to be a powerful leader. And when Lord Fujikawa had started talking of war, he had wanted to fight rather than talk.

But now instead of thinking of glory on the battlefield, his thoughts were filled with Yuki. Her smile and her laugh. What a fool he'd been to open his heart.

Twinkling bells chimed in the garden and Hotaru heaved a sigh. *Not now.*

There was no avoiding her. She was critical in winning the war. Hotaru hauled himself to his feet and went to meet the witch. When he stepped into the garden, however, it was not the old witch who greeted him, but a beautiful young woman with long raven hair and a crescent-shaped scar by her eye.

"Who are you?"

"Do you not recognize me? I am your wife."

"You're not Yuki." Hotaru glanced over his shoulder, searching for a weapon. Had the monster from the Fujimori's survived and followed him here?

The young woman laughed, and her voice was soft and sweet. "You're correct, that girl is gone."

"What happened to her?"

"It does not matter. You have your alliance, and your bride." She touched his arm but he jerked his hand away.

"If what you're saying is true, then Yuki is—" He choked on his words. He never should have left her behind. What if that creature hadn't been the only one trying to kill her?

"You fell in love with her, didn't you? Fool, I thought you were smarter than this."

It was as if the wind had been knocked out him. He stumbled and almost fell over, and leaned on the nearby wall. "How did this happen?"

She arched an eyebrow. "You wanted to win this war, more than anything. For your own vanity."

He stared at the young woman, eyes wide. "No."

"I told you my power was depleted. And when I ordered you to marry the girl, you never questioned me."

"NO!" he shouted as he shook his head. "Not like this. That's not what I asked for!"

"It was your own willful ignorance that destroyed her."

Hotaru's entire body trembled with rage. An animalistic growl burst from him as he as he ran for his sword. He lunged at the witch, but before he could even land a blow she leaped out of his way.

"Do you think you're any match for me boy?" she taunted.

"I'll kill you."

"And for one woman, you would doom your people? I have the ear of each clan leader, all of them belong to me. If you turn on me now, I will exterminate the Kaedemoris and they will be nothing but a distant memory."

Hotaru hesitated. He'd seen what she could do, it was no idle threat. His hubris had brought them here, and there was no changing the past. Yuki was dead, but he could spare his people.

"I will end this war today. You've done well so far. Together we can reach for greater heights. Just take my hand."

Hotaru took a shaking step toward her, his feet like lead, and his sword hung loosely at his side. She smiled at him in triumph as he took her hand.

"You're doing the right thing," she said.

Hotaru plunged his sword into her heart. "I would rather die than join Yuki's murderer."

Blood poured from the wound and she stumbled away from him, clutching the sword which was embedded in her chest. With both hands she yanked it free and dropped it to the floor. A trickle of blood seeped from it as the wound knitted itself closed. But as it did, the color started to fade from her hair and gray streaks showed through the black. Crow's feet crept in around her eyes.

She might not be entirely human but she was not without limitless energy. She could be killed. He lunged for her again, prepared to strangle her with his own two hands if he must. She ran away from him, out into the courtyard. He chased her but she disappeared in a puff of smoke.

When she was gone, he collapsed onto his knees, overcome by

grief. Head tilted backward, staring up at the gray sky, he unleashed a horrible shout, a mangled sound that brought his servants running to him.

He had left Yuki behind because he thought he was protecting her. Instead he had doomed her with his own selfishness.

28

The shrine sat on top of a hill, guarded by barren trees which stood like sentinels along the perimeter. The bright red rooftops were a beacon against the otherwise barren landscape. Crisp white ofuda hung from the tori arches and fluttered in the breeze. The temple had been transformed over winter, and here the first hints of spring could be seen. Green buds were waiting to burst to life along the trees.

A woman with auburn hair swept the main courtyard, humming to herself as she worked. At a glance her fox ears blended in with her auburn hair. The hair was unusual in itself, and most visitors to this foothill shrine never saw her at all. The only reason he could see her in her real form was because he knew the truth about her. She turned as she swept and caught sight of him.

"Hotaru, what brings you here? The spring festival isn't for another couple weeks." Seeing as he was alone, she frowned.

Seeing his brother's wife reminded him of what he'd lost and grief burned deep in his gut. His throat was tight. Coming here was difficult. Hotaru had taken the rule of the Kaedemori clan from his older brother. Though they'd made peace between them, they'd never been close. He had to swallow his pride to ask for help. He'd tried doing everything on his own and it had gotten Yuki killed. If anyone knew how to defeat the witch, it would be Rin.

"I need your help." The words got tangled in his throat.

Rin tilted her head in confusion. "You need my help?"

"What is this, brother?" Hikaru strode forward, wearing the white haori and black hakama of a priest, and a tall black hat on top of his head. In one hand he held a branch. Hotaru must have interrupted a ceremony of some kind. He couldn't face Hikaru, knowing what a mess he'd made of things for the clan since he'd taken over.

"Nothing." Hotaru turned to leave.

Hikaru chased after him, grabbing him by the arm to keep him from leaving.

"You wouldn't have come here if it was nothing," Hikaru said.

Hotaru took a deep breath and then fell to his knees on the cold stones, his head parallel to the ground.

"I am a wretch who doesn't deserve your kindness, but I have a favor to ask of you."

Hikaru waved his hands. "There's no need for this." He grabbed Hotaru by the shoulders and guided him to stand. "You're my brother, you don't need to beg me to assist you."

"I've made a terrible mistake." Hotaru kept his head lowered. "I made a deal with a witch to try and protect the clan." He caught himself and then corrected, "Lord Fujikawa came to me after his daughter disappeared. He wanted answers and I had none. Things escalated from there and we're at war. I made a deal with a witch to defeat him and she—" Hotaru choked on the next words. "She killed the woman I loved in exchange for power."

Complete silence followed. The only sound was the whistle of the wind. Hikaru would likely deny him. His greed should be punished. This was Hotaru's fault after all. Had he not desired what did not belong to him, the clan would not be in danger.

Hikaru squeezed his shoulder. "I think we need to talk."

Hotaru lifted his head. Rin frowned. Hikaru rubbed the back of his neck. They brought him into their home where Hikaru served him tea. Rin sat to one side, glaring at him. He didn't blame her. Once the tea things were set out, Hikaru took a seat across from him.

"I think there are things you ought to know."

Hikaru shared his story, about the witch and her plot to destroy their family. And like a fool, Hotaru had fallen right into her trap. It seemed she had been plaguing their family for generations.

"This war is partially my fault. I should have intervened sooner..." Hikaru trailed off.

"But you're no longer an elder!" Hotaru protested.

Hikaru shook his head. "I ran away from my duty, and left you with the burden. It wasn't fair. I will plead with the forest guardian Akio, whom I serve. He will give our clan protection, but it will come at a price."

"What sort of price?"

Hikaru waved his hands in front of him frantically. "Nothing serious. He will likely want the family to make him their deity. We would be expected to give offering to him."

"Done. Whatever it takes to keep the family safe from the witch." His stomach twisted with worry. He trusted Hikaru's judgment, but he couldn't help but wonder if he were making the right choice. He'd been wrong before.

"I'm sorry. I should have been there for you," Hikaru said, placing his hand on his shoulder.

Hotaru stared at the cook-fire in front of him. "I wanted to lead; this is the cost. I'll find a way." Hotaru looked into his teacup. Steam rose in thick tendrils up from it. The clan would find a way, they always had. But would he ever recover from the loss of Yuki?

Hotaru headed back to the palace on foot. The sun was starting to set and the sky was painted with reds and oranges. He thought back to that day in the forest with Yuki and grief washed over him once more. Like a punch to the gut, he stumbled a bit and leaned against a nearby tree, taking a shuddering breath. Only when he was alone would he let the loss overwhelm him.

He took a moment to compose himself and grasped onto the tree trunk tightly. As he stood upright once again, he noticed a tanuki sitting along the side of the road. It was a ragged mess, its fur tangled and dirty. But despite that, it stared at him with clever black eyes.

"Are you one of hers?" he asked.

The tanuki watched him, unblinking. *I'm being ridiculous, they couldn't have followed me here. And besides, she's dead.* He kept walking back toward the palace, but as he did, the tanuki limped along after him. He turned around and stared at the tanuki who stared back.

"What do you want? I already know she's dead. Don't come here and taunt me."

The creature did not respond. He picked up a nearby rock and tossed it at it. The animal did not budge, even when the rock nearly grazed its head. Hotaru ran toward it, flapping his arms. It scurried off then, into the nearby bushes. Hotaru watched it walk away, his heart constricting. He took a few steps before turning back around to see the tanuki lying in the middle of the road.

Without a second thought he rushed over to it, picking it up in his arms. The animal was breathing heavy, and seemed to have been wounded by something. The palace was far away, and no place for a wild animal. Perhaps if he brought it to the shrine? This might be his last link to Yuki. He couldn't let it die.

Hotaru ran back to the shrine with the tanuki cradled in his arms. As he arrived in the courtyard, Rin and Hikaru came out.

Rin saw it straight away. "What happened to this child?" She took the small tanuki into her arms. The animal raised its nose and growled. Rin nodded her head as the animal spoke in some way only she could understand.

"That's not a regular tanuki then?" Hotaru asked.

Hikaru watched the conversation between Rin and the tanuki, his head tilted to the side as he frowned and tried to discern what was being said.

The tanuki finished speaking and Rin said to Hotaru, "He came here to find you. He says Yuki is alive and she needs your help."

"Who's Yuki?" Hikaru asked.

Hotaru ignored him and moved closer to the tanuki. Hope was blooming in him again. "She's alive? Where is she?"

Rin put her ear closer to the tanuki. It had closed its eyes again and was breathing slowly. Its voice was barely a squeak.

When he was done speaking, Rin said, "He says at the guardian's place. I don't know what that is."

"I do," Hotaru replied.

He ran for the stairs as his brother called out to him. Yuki was alive!

29

It took nearly a day to get to the hidden forest shrine. Riding through the night, he nearly exhausted his horse in the process. The day was dying as he arrived, and the sound of night insects filled the air. Hotaru approached the water where the guardian's shrine stood.

Floating on the surface of the water was a small boat made of twisted vines, and tethered in place by reeds. A latticework of branches covered the top, and he could see a small flash of white beneath it.

The remaining six tanuki sat at the water's edge, kneeling in prayer, their tiny paws pressed together and their heads bowed. When they noticed him, they swarmed around him, their small voices chirping.

"Save her!" they cried.

Now that he was closer, he could see Yuki's profile through the branches. She lay as if sleeping, hands folded on her stomach. Pale and serene. Seeing her like that felt like a punch to the gut. He had done this to her, but perhaps there was something he could do to reverse it.

Hotaru gently pushed aside the tanuki before wading into the water toward Yuki. The glowing lights he had seen before swirled around her sleeping form, but as he got closer they scattered and hovered just over his head like hundreds of twinkling lights.

The gaps between the branches were small, and he could barely fit his arm through. He cupped her cheek and found it was ice cold.

"How do I wake her?" he asked the tanuki.

"She's lost her spark," one of the tanuki chirped.

"You have to find the spark!" a second added.

The tanuki continued their chatter but none of it made sense. He would find the witch and destroy her if that was what it took. He brushed his hand against her cheek. *I am sorry for everything Yuki. I'll do anything to make this right.*

"Do you sincerely mean that?" a voice brushed against his skin.

The guardian sat on the top of the shrine. His outline was pale and translucent, made up by the hundreds of floating lights which all coalesced into one place.

"I would do anything to save her," Hotaru replied.

The guardian regarded him for a moment, his expression bland. From what Yuki told him, he often ignored her cries for help. But he had to help. They were one, weren't they?

"The witch has stolen my energy out of her, and it cannot be recovered. The witch is already beyond your reach."

"I'll chase her to the ends of the earth if that's what it takes," Hotaru replied.

The guardian shook his head. "Yuki's time already runs short. She will not make it to the next sunrise."

"You have to do something! You saved her once, can't you do it again?"

He shook his head, the blue lights dancing around him as he did. "I cannot spare her. I gave up my earthly body to save her once. Now in the heavenly realm, I can only guide you."

"What can we do?"

"You must think hard on your choice. There is no going back once it is done."

"Whatever it is, I will do it."

"This child should never have lived. It was my divine spark that kept her in the mortal realm. But with it gone, her soul's fire is dying. The only thing that can save her is if it is reignited."

"How do I do that?"

"You must give up your own."

All the air came out of him in a rush. Either live without Yuki or die himself. He'd already felt what it was to lose her. He never wanted to experience that sort of pain again.

"How?"

The vines peeled backward, revealing Yuki lying on a bed of leaves, her ebony hair splayed around her.

"Breathe into her, and I shall do the rest," the guardian replied.

The guardian's form flickered and disappeared. Hotaru was left alone, waist deep in the water, his fingers curled around the edge of the boat.

He leaned forward and cupped her cheek, admiring her face and the soft brush of her eyelashes against her cheek. Her ruby red lips.

"I love you, Yuki." He pressed his lips to hers and he felt the breath of life escape him, flowing into Yuki.

As air filled her lungs, she gasped and her eyes flung open. Hotaru stared down at her, but already the darkness had begun to creep in around his vision. His hands were numb and he couldn't feel her skin against his fingertips.

"Hotaru?"

Their eyes met for one brief moment. It was worth it to see her one last time.

"Goodbye, Yuki," he said before he collapsed into the ground, water filled his lungs. As he lost consciousness he heard Yuki shouting his name over and over.

Live long and live well, my heart.

Yuki sat up. The boat she was lying in almost tipped over as she reached for Hotaru, who dipped down beneath the water. She clung onto him, pulling him into the boat with her.

She shook him. "Hotaru, wake up." But there was no response.

The tanuki were leaping up and down along the shore. She scanned her surroundings. What was she doing here?

"What did you do?" A tear rolled down her cheek. All she had wanted was to forget. The release of death had almost been welcome. And yet here he was, lifeless in her arms.

"He has given his life for yours," the guardian said.

Yuki turned toward him. The guardian was a pale, shimmering specter floating a few feet away.

"Why would he do such a stupid thing?" She brushed the hair away from his face, and stared into his slack expression as he grew colder.

"Because he loved you and he regretted what he did to you. This was his way of making amends."

"This can't be how it ends." Yuki turned to the guardian. "I can't let him die."

The guardian gave her a sad smile. "Both of you cannot live. Your life was given to you by my power, without it you were dying. He gave his life to you, so that you may live."

Yuki shook her head.

"I'm going to give it back then. I don't want it."

She leaned downward, pressing her lips against Hotaru's. They were cold and stiff. Hot tears rolled down her cheeks as she clung onto his lifeless body.

Don't leave me. I love you.

The forest was silent, not even the wind blew through the trees. Very faintly, Yuki felt the heartbeat of the trees, the song of the birds, the earth beneath her. A small part of the guardian remained in her, but it was only a speck. The witch hadn't taken it all.

In her mind's eye, she cupped that speck in her hands and held it close. *Please, help me save him.* Then like a seed burst from the soil it grew inside her, spreading outward, branching into every part of her. As the power grew it moved through her filling her with the guardian's holy energy. And then it poured out of Yuki past her lips and filled Hotaru's lungs.

He gasped and started to breathe again, though he did not regain consciousness. Yuki sat back, looking at the slow rise and fall of Hotaru's chest. Her eyes were covered with a gold sheen that was already starting to fade.

"I did it!" She cheered and looked toward the guardian. She could hardly see him at all now, he was nothing but a faint glimmer.

"My last gift to you, the seed of life. Now and forever your souls shall be bound together. Live well, Yuki, live well."

Along the shore, the tanuki waved at her as they too faded from view. To save him, she used the last of the guardian's power and along with it her connection to the world of kami and yokai.

30

The ever-present feeling of oneness with the forest was gone, and as much as she mourned it, she was more relieved Hotaru lived. From the moment Hotaru had taken his first breath after she'd breathed life into him again, she felt his heartbeat echoing inside her chest. The guardian and the forest's presence had been replaced by Hotaru. Memories and images swirled around in her brain, replacing her awareness of the forest. It felt like she was in a waking dream. She wasn't sure what was real and what was fantasy.

Yuki paced outside the healer's room. She'd been too under-foot and had been evicted. The door slid open and the healer came out. Yuki rushed toward him.

"How is he? Has he wakened yet? You can't keep me out."

He held up his hand to stop her barrage of questions in their tracks.

"You can go in now, he's awake," he said with the shake of his head.

She almost knocked the healer over in her haste to get to Hotaru.

Hotaru was sitting up, his face pale but he was alive and

breathing. She flung herself into his arms. They collided and he made a soft oof.

She clung onto him as if were she to let him go she'd wake up in the forest once more, with his dead body in her arms.

"Yuki, I can't breathe," he gasped.

She eased off him and laced her fingers together to avoid the urge to grab a hold of him. His discomfort washed over her and multiplied within her. She was confused by the reaction.

"I didn't know you'd be coming to visit. I would have dressed up," he said, trying to lighten the tension.

He'd sacrificed himself to save her. She knew he loved her, but his emotions confused her. And she realized this connection might be unwanted by him. They'd parted on bad terms and there was so much left unsaid, where did they even begin?

"Not that I'm ungrateful, but how is it that I'm breathing right now?"

Yuki kept her gaze on the blankets over Hotaru's knee.

"I couldn't let you die for me, so I tried to give you back the breath of life. And well..."

"I was trying to be heroic you know." He grabbed her chin and tilted her head up to meet his gaze.

His eyes were different from before. There was a golden ring around the outer edge, just like hers.

"Why did you do it?" she asked, but it felt like a stupid question.

"I think you know why. Just like I know why you really saved my life."

She bit her lip. So the memories and feelings went both ways.

"What are we?" She asked.

Hotaru sighed. "I was hoping you knew?"

They were husband and wife. Their life bound in more ways than one. She hadn't even given him the choice. And now she'd lost her connection to the forest as well. They were forever entwined. There was no knowing how deep this connection went.

Her thoughts might never be her own again. A sudden wave of anxiety washed over her and she found it difficult to breathe.

He placed his hand on hers and squeezed. "It's going to be alright."

His touch soothed her and she took a deep breath.

"Before, the guardian lived inside me. I could feel the forest, and I sensed his presence when he was near. But I cannot see him or the tanuki anymore. I used the last of his power to split your soul between us." She paused to fidget with the hem of her haori. "I can sense you and your heartbeat the way I did the forest."

"I guess I had enough energy to share. Maybe that's why that yokai was after me." He chuckled.

Yuki laughed as well. And then awkward silence filled the room.

"I know how you feel about me," Hotaru said. "But I also know you're afraid of being tied down. I won't force you—" Before he could finish his sentence, she leaned forward and kissed him. It was easier to use her body to speak for her rather than words.

Hotaru smiled against her lips. "I was hoping you'd say that."

She pulled back but kept her arms around his neck. "Even if we weren't soul bonded, I would choose you. I never should have let you go."

He leaned his forehead against hers. "I'm sorry I took the forest from you."

She shook her head. "I chose you over the forest. That's all I ever wanted was the choice."

He kissed her again, deepening it, his hands caressing her body. "We still haven't had a wedding night."

She laughed as he pulled the covers over the pair of them.

It was several more days of convalescence, and quite a few secret rendezvous with furtive kisses before they could be officially together as husband and wife. Normally when a pair were wed, they'd present themselves to the elder of the clan. Because Riku had been sick during their wedding, they hadn't had the chance. Before Yuki could start her life with Hotaru, they'd have to take this step. She had thought Riku would do away with formalities.

Much to her discomfort, her brother had them present themselves in full ceremony before the entire clan. Her brother's health had improved greatly since the yokai had been killed. On a steady diet and being free of their stepmother's spell had helped him fill out. He waited for them seated on the dais. He looked very much like her late father, and she did a double take upon entering. The clan was gathered around silent and solemn.

When Riku had first taken over the rule of the clan, he had often appeared meek and shrunken. But now he looked powerful and wise. He watched the pair of them as they approached. Yuki wore a bright, colorful kimono, and Hotaru was in a matching haori and hakama. They knelt down in front of him, falling into a deep bow as was expected. It was out of character for her to rely on ceremony, but she hoped by playing by the rules they'd get her brother's blessing, but she couldn't leave the clan until she did.

Hotaru, sensing her fear, reached over and gave her hand a subtle squeeze. It was going to take time to get used to having her thoughts and feelings exposed to another. But it was nice to have him there to support her without asking. Her brother noticed and cleared his throat in disapproval.

"Lord Kademori, you plotted to take control of my clan and put my sister's life at risk," he said, listing Hotaru's crimes.

Yuki looked to her brother with pleading eyes. "Brother, please. I've explained it to you already!"

He made a slashing movement with his hand to silence her.

"You're no more innocent. You knew what he was after from the start and went along with it. Then you went missing for days, and I thought you were dead." His voice caught, and Yuki saw a hint of the brother she knew. This wasn't about the marriage, she'd worried him.

"I'm sorry." Yuki bowed her head lower.

"Yuki is the heart of the household. I would rather not see her go."

Hotaru looked at Riku with sincerity in his gaze. "I came here searching for an alliance. But if you will let me have her, then I can ask nothing else of you."

Riku stared at her for a moment. Then he said, "Answer me one question. Do you love him, Yuki?"

Yuki took her husband's hand and squeezed it. "With all my heart."

Her brother's shoulders relaxed as did his stern expression. "I promised you that you could marry the man you loved. You have my blessing."

Yuki leaped up to hug her brother tight, ceremony be damned. She grabbed onto him, and for the first time in a long time, his strong arms wrapped around her, holding her tight. She would miss him and the only place that had been her home.

"Father would have been proud," he said in her ear.

"Thank you, brother." She had to struggle to fight the tears that came to her eyes.

Then her brother slipped a necklace into her hand. Her mother's necklace. She hadn't seen it since she threw it at Riku's feet.

"This belongs to you. There will always be a place for you here in the forest."

Yuki's hand closed around the necklace. Even if she no longer felt the forest inside her, it was always there with her.

EPILOGUE

The forest was still, the pond motionless. Not even a single leaf fell to disturb the surface of the water. It was as if the place was frozen in time.

Though the weight of the child she carried was great, and getting up and down was getting more difficult each day, still Yuki knelt by the waterside. She pressed her hands together in prayer.

I know you cannot reveal yourself to me any longer, but I came to say thank you. For everything. I never realized how precious life was until I had one growing inside me.

The wind rustled through the trees and Yuki looked up. A single, glowing light bobbed on the air in front of her, and she smiled.

"The war is over; the clans have come to a truce. Thanks to the guardian Akio we are safe from the witch. She has fled far away, though no one knows where she went." She told him as if the kami cared at all about the dealings of humans.

Her knees were getting wet from crouching down so long on the bank of the pond. She groaned and started to rise. But as she did, Hotaru came up behind her, putting his hand on the small of her back.

"I'm fine." She playfully smacked at his arm.

"I may have indulged you in coming here when you're this pregnant, but I'm not going to stand by while my wife struggles to stand."

She stuck her tongue out at him and he only shook his head. She liked to pretend she didn't need his help. But he knew of course. They'd learned ways to keep things from one another, but she found little need for it now. Their bond, especially while she was pregnant, had only grown stronger.

But as their child grew inside her, she was forced to get help more often than she liked to admit. The closer to her time she got, the more restless she became. She often thought of her mother, who'd died giving birth to her, and she longed for the forest and the reassurance of the guardian. Though her connection with it and him were gone, she liked to think he still cared about her.

"I don't think he heard me," Yuki remarked as Hotaru guided her from the clearing.

"I think he heard. He may no longer be a part of you but he's always watching."

Yuki leaned onto her husband's shoulder. "Perhaps you're right," she said. "I wish I could have seen the tanuki again though."

"Me too," he said, placing a kiss on her forehead.

The pair of them walked away, and unseen to them, the guardian sat on top of his shrine, a smile on his face. The tanuki also gathered along the shore, surrounding the place she had been. They'd gathered around her while she prayed, invisible to her now that she had lost the sight. A few wiped tears from their eyes. It had been a difficult transition for them losing their playmate, but such was the course of nature. The yokai and kami lived in a time and place outside that of the humans. The Lord of Animals had known it was time for her to rejoin her own kind. Though it pained him that they must conceal themselves from her, it was a comfort to see she'd found happiness at last.

"You've done well, child," he said.

Yuki, almost out of sight, turned toward him and tilted her head to the side. Her eyes were searching for what she could not see. Hotaru watched her, his face beaming with love.

"I thought I heard something, but perhaps it was the wind." She turned away and walked hand in hand with her husband.

THE STORY CONTINUES IN...

If you enjoyed this retelling check out the next book in the series, Okami: A Little Red Ridinghood Retelling.

A charming wolf falls in love with a his enemies grandaughter and must choose between revenge and love.

Get it here.

Want even more stories in the Land of Akatsuki? Get The Priestess and the Dragon, Book One in the Dragon Saga for free Get your copy today!

ALSO BY NICOLETTE ANDREWS

World of Akatsuki

The Dragon Saga:

The Priestess and the Dragon

The Sea Stone

The Song of the Wind

The Fractured Soul

The Immortal Vow

Tales of Akatsuki

Kitsune: A Little Mermaid Retelling

Yuki: A Snow White Retelling

Okami: A Little Red Ridinghood retelling

Diviner's World

Duchess

Diviner's Prophecy

Diviner's Curse

Diviner's Fate

Princess

Thornwood Series

Heart of Thorns

Tangled in Thorns

Daughter of Thorns

Queen of Thorns

ABOUT THE AUTHOR

Nicolette is a native San Diegan with a passion for the world of make believe. From a young age, Nicolette was telling stories whether it be writing plays for her friends to act out or making a series of children's books that her mother still likes drag out to embarrass her with in front of company. She still lives in her imagination but in reality she resides in San Diego with her husband, children and a couple cats. She loves reading, attempting arts and crafts, and cooking.

You can visit her at her website: www.fantasyauthornicoletteandrews.com or at these places: